Trapped by Impulsion

CHARLES FEGGANS

Copyright © 2024 Charles Feggans.

All rights reserved. No part of this book may be reproduced, stored, or transmitted by any means—whether auditory, graphic, mechanical, or electronic—without written permission of both publisher and author, except in the case of brief excerpts used in critical articles and reviews. Unauthorized reproduction of any part of this work is illegal and is punishable by law.

ISBN: 979-8-89419-221-5 (sc)
ISBN: 979-8-89419-222-2 (hc)
ISBN: 979-8-89419-223-9 (e)

Because of the dynamic nature of the Internet, any web addresses or links contained in this book may have changed since publication and may no longer be valid. The views expressed in this work are solely those of the author and do not necessarily reflect the views of the publisher, and the publisher hereby disclaims any responsibility for them.

One Galleria Blvd., Suite 1900, Metairie, LA 70001
(504) 702-6708

Force into running drugs for prison inmates, Jack Wilson got the shaft…and took the fall!

When Jack Wilson was laid off from his job three years earlier, his family fell on hard times. A good job was hard to find, and eventually his long search took him to a state correctional facility.

Before Jack knew it, he was plunged headlong into the cut-throat world of double-dealing, crime, and depravity among the hardened inmates of the prison.

Jack's co-workers were anything but your average stiffs. They were inmates who knew how to pull the right strings to get what they wanted. And what they wanted most were drugs. Forced into this precarious trap, Jack begins making drug pick-ups outside of the prison. With the instructions and contacts of certain inmates, Jack learned how to smuggle large quantities of contraband into the high-security building.

A FEW WORDS FROM THE AUTHOR

As you read this story, keep in mind that what happened to Jack could happen to anyone. It didn't necessarily have to take place in a prison. It could have happened on the job, at a friend's home, or almost anywhere else.

This story is directed toward drug involvement. It is designed to give the average reader an idea of what really happens to dealers, traffickers and persons who choose to be associated with its environment from a point of view where money and mental attitude is concerned.

Naturally, their families may be placed in a position to suffer as well. They could be parents, spouse, children, or close relatives. Let us take a look at the children after it has been known that a member of that family is involved with drugs.

They may be avoided by important friends or picked on by those who are pressured to harass them. This may lead to loneliness and despair. These mental images of the ideal mother, father, siblings or relatives may deteriorate as well. This scare may bring about a long-lasting effects.

From the point of view of the spouse of a drug handler, he or she stands a chance of losing status within the community, his/her social environment, relatives, and not to say the least, friends.

As far as friends are concerned, this may draw the line as to who are your true friends, the ones you can count on for support as opposed to the ones who will turn their backs to you. The idea of a true friend is someone who will always be there, regardless of the situation until the crime is proven to be horrifying.

If this story should happen to a son or daughter, brother or sister, they face the chance of having their future altered and possibly destroyed. It could leave them with a police record for life which would eliminate them from certain professions and careers.

Parents may tend to disown their child. Most don't have the funds for bail. Hardship may be placed on them if they have to borrow money or refinance property to gather the necessary bail.

My final words to the reader: Today is the first day of the rest of your life. Don't let anyone pressure or persuade you into destroying the rest of it.

A FEW WORDS FROM THE AUTHOR

As you read this story, keep in mind that what happened to Jack could happen to anyone. It didn't necessarily have to take place in a prison. It could have happened on the job, at a friend's home, or almost anywhere else.

This story is directed toward drug involvement. It is designed to give the average reader an idea of what really happens to dealers, traffickers and persons who choose to be associated with its environment from a point of view where money and mental attitude is concerned.

Naturally, their families may be placed in a position to suffer as well. They could be parents, spouse, children, or close relatives. Let us take a look at the children after it has been known that a member of that family is involved with drugs.

They may be avoided by important friends or picked on by those who are pressured to harass them. This may lead to loneliness and despair. These mental images of the ideal mother, father, siblings or relatives may deteriorate as well. This scare may bring about a long-lasting effects.

From the point of view of the spouse of a drug handler, he or she stands a chance of losing status within the community, his/her social environment, relatives, and not to say the least, friends.

As far as friends are concerned, this may draw the line as to who are your true friends, the ones you can count on for support as opposed to the ones who will turn their backs to you. The idea of a true friend is someone who will always be there, regardless of the situation until the crime is proven to be horrifying.

If this story should happen to a son or daughter, brother or sister, they face the chance of having their future altered and possibly destroyed. It could leave them with a police record for life which would eliminate them from certain professions and careers.

Parents may tend to disown their child. Most don't have the funds for bail. Hardship may be placed on them if they have to borrow money or refinance property to gather the necessary bail.

My final words to the reader: Today is the first day of the rest of your life. Don't let anyone pressure or persuade you into destroying the rest of it.

CHAPTER ONE

7:25 a.m.

My wife was half-dressed, standing in front of the bedroom mirror combing her hair. She had just gotten out of the shower a few minutes earlier. The two children, Bill and Sam, were in their own rooms dressing for school. I was still lying in bed sleeping.

The doorbell rang. As I was being awakened by the ringing sound, I could hear my son Bill saying there was someone at the door through the talking of "Good Morning America" on the bedroom television. My wife went to the bathroom window to look out. The bathroom window was overlooking the driveway on the second level facing the street. A gray, late model car sat at the edge of the driveway, not on it. By this time, the doorbell rang again. She came back into the bedroom and began to shake me. "Jack, Jack. There's someone at the door with a gray car," she was saying as I started slowly rolling out of the bed. I reached for my trousers that was lying on the seat of a green, cushioned chair next to my night stand. The doorbell rang again. I pulled my trousers over to me and hastily pulled them up. As I walked toward the door, I snapped the waist band and pulled up my zipper. Than I walked down the six steps to the door with sleep still in my eyes. I unlocked the top latch and turned the knob directly underneath it. Then I pulled the door open.

The sun was shining brightly. Its shadow was casting over the front steps and part of the driveway. The grass was still wet from the morning dew. The sound of birds could be heard in the nearby trees chirping various morning calls. The air was still. No traffic was moving up or down this dead-end street which my home was facing.

Before me on the landing stood a dark-skinned man in a dark blue work jacket and matching trousers. I recognized him as the man who was at my door exactly two weeks earlier. He had introduced himself as Joe. As I let him enter my home, he began talking about what a fine day it was and what he should be doing. I made a related comment. I walked up the six steps leading to the upper level. At the top of the steps, I noticed to my left, at the far end of the short hallway, my wife shutting the door to our bedroom. I waved for Joe to come up. He did and followed me into the kitchen. Once inside, I turned to face him as he entered.

"I called your house a couple times in the past two weeks," he said. "No one answered. Later, I remembered you telling me you would be home in the mornings up until 10 a.m. So I decided to stop by to pick up some of the same stuff you sold to me the last time I was here. I hope you remembered I said I would be back in two weeks to pick up a quarter. Do you have it?"

"Yeah." I walked to the cabinets over top of the refrigerator, pulled out a small brown bag which contained four ounces of weed and laid it on the counter next to the refrigerator for him to check it out. He picked it up, examined it and returned it to the counter. "That's what I'm talking about," he said.

"Nothing but the best for my customers," I added. I opened the door to another cabinet which was about 18 inches away on my left, took out a small glass and immediately went to the refrigerator to grab a container of orange juice. As I did so, I turned to Joe and asked him if he wanted a glass. He replied, "No."

I proceeded to pour a glass for myself.

All of a sudden Joe said, "I know I asked you to save me four ounces. Well, my friends only want two ounces. That's all the money they gave me for the purchase."

"That's okay. Joe. I'll tell you what I'll do. I'll give you all four ounces now and when you get the rest of the money, come by and drop it off. If I'm not here, put the money under the door mat. Leave a note in the mail box saying you left it. I'll know it was you who left it."

"What if they don't want to be responsible for the other two ounces? Why don't you hold onto it?"

I paused for a minute. Still holding a half-gallon of orange juice, I filled a small glass. Then I put the container back into the refrigerator. I turned to Joe and looked him straight into his eyes while I place the glass on the counter. "Joe. I think I can trust you with this other two ounces. Take it. I don't want it laying around the house. Give me what money you have."

Joe handed over the $150 and I counted it in his presence. I then picked up the small brown bag and handed it to him. He took the bag, opened it again. Took the contents out. "You sure you want to do this?" He asked.

"Yeah," I replied.

He put it back into its bag and with a nod of his head, he started toward the front door. I followed close closely behind him.

"I'll get back in touch with you later," he said. He exit and I watched as he walked down the driveway, climbed into his vehicle and drove away. I didn't give the deal another though as I locked the door and headed back toward my bedroom. Not bothering to remove my trousers, I laid on the bed with the intentions of going back to sleep.

By now, my wife Jane was fully dressed. She was wearing a pair of green pants with a white belt, an open face blouse and her sneakers had the appearance of being worn for the very first time. My two sons came into the room at the same time to get their hair combed. As my wife started to tend to their hair, she said to me in a quiet voice, "Was that one of your friends who calls here all the time?"

"Yeah." I responded.

"What did he want?"

"Nothing important. Just some business we had planned." I continued to lay on the bed with my eyes half closed. "Good Morning America" was the only sound that could be heard.

CHAPTER TWO

As Joe rounded the corner from the street where he had just picked up the weed. He called into headquarters from just two blocks away.

"Sgt. Jerone, this is Joe." He said over his car radio.

A voice came back saying, "Go Joe."

"I just picked up the package. I'll be there in about three or four minutes." Joe drove to Headquarters. There he immediately got out of his unmarked vehicle with the package in his hand and went into Sgt. Jerone's office.

Sgt. Jerone had been with the Narcotics Division for almost ten years. He travels throughout the state with his team of five state troopers cracking down on drug activities. In the hallway leading to Sgt. Jerone's office, the walls on both sides were lined with his men and three plain-cloth local police officers waiting to act on Sgt. Jerone's command.

Joe entered Sgt. Jerone's office and laid the small brown bag on his desk. Sgt. Jerone opened the bag, looked over the contents. Paused for a moment then looked up at Joe. "Thanks Joe." He got up from his chair, shook Joe's hand. "Is there anything to report?"

"Well, the only people in the house are his kids, his wife and himself. He doesn't appear to have any guns. I think he gave me all the stuff that was in the house. Also, he's half dressed."

Sgt. Jerone walked past Joe and into the hallway. He stopped to take a quick look at his men. He told them to get into four unmarked cars waiting outside the building,

The four cars proceeded to the street where the bag had been picked up. When they reached the corner, the lead car stopped. Sgt. Jerone got out. He gave instructions to everyone inside the cars except the drivers. Then he went to the back of his car, took out two slug jammers. He kept one for himself and gave another to one of the plain-clothes Officers. In an easy tone of voice, he instructed the other seven men to proceed on foot so as to not cause any suspicion.

The officers walked the six hundred feet to the property. Near the edge of the driveway, Sgt. Jerone ordered two plain-clothes officers to go around to the back of the house with a slug hammer. With a wave of his hand, the other officers quietly walked up to the front steps. He and one other officer proceeded toward the top. One step from the top Sgt. Jerone stopped to ready his slug hammer. The other officer opened the storm door and waited. The remaining officers who were standing-by moved in close to the garage so as not to be detected by anyone looking out their windows. The officer near the front door was ordered to ring the doorbell.

8:07 a.m.

The doorbell rang again. I was still lying in bed watching television. My son Bill ran to the bath room window to look out. Jane continued to fix her hair. Sam was sitting on the edge of the bed watching television. Bill came back into the room. "Mom, that car is out there again," he said.

Immediately she went into the bath room. The bell rang again. Jane came back into the bed room. Upon entering, she said, "Jack, there's a gray car out by the driveway. I can't see who's at the door. Can you see who's there?"

I got up and proceeded toward the door. My son Sam started to run past me saying, "I'll get it."

Immediately Jane called out, "Sam, come back here. Get in this room and shut the door."

I could hear the door close as I walked down the six steps to the front door. Just as I put my hand on the door knob, the bell rang again. I turned the knob and pulled the door wide open. A man stood directly in front of me wearing regular street clothes. Instantly he flashed a badge in my face.

"You know the deal," he said. Immediately he rushed into the house. Sgt. Jerone ran in right behind him. The four under-covers who were standing next to the garage door rushed up the steps and into the house. One of these officers ran up the inside home steps. The other three ran down the inside steps. The man with the badge and Sgt. Jerone stayed near me. Sgt. Jerone put the slug hammer down. In a mild tone of voice, he said, "In about another two seconds, we were ready to break the door in. The reason we held off, we got word that there was small kids in here."

I was asked to go upstairs and take a seat. Two officers escorted me to the dining room table. I pulled out a chair and took a seat as directed. Both officers also pulled out a chair on my left and right and sat next to me.

The bedroom door opened. I could hear my wife talking to the kids and the television still playing. Sgt. Jerone told one of his men to go talk to my wife. The officer walked to the bedroom. The door was slightly opened. He knocked on it. Jane pulled it open. He walked in. Slowly closing it behind him. The kids and Jane were now staring at him.

"There is an investigation going on," he said. "I want you to take the kids and leave. From what we know so far, you don't know anything about what's going on. For you, it would be better this way. We are interested in your husband only for now."

The two officers who were at the back of the house now came in through the front door. The officers who were down stairs came up stairs to be with the other two officers. Together, all the men stood next to the wall separating the dining room from the kitchen. They didn't want the kids to see them and get upset.

Jane got her coat. Then she got the boy's coats. She made no comment as she turned off the television. All four of them walked down the steps toward the garage. As she was leaving, I saw her look in my direction. She had a look of sadness written across her face. The boys were quiet. They had a neutral expression on their face. When they reached the bottom, all turned left. She opened the door wide leading to the garage and upon entering, pressed the control on the wall to let the overhead door up.

In the meantime, the four cars had parked in the driveway. She asked the officer with her if they could move the cars so she could get out. The officer stood motionless for about a minute. Then he called up to Sgt. Jerone asking if he should search the car. Sgt. Jerone replied that it was okay to let her out. She made the kids get into the car. The two cars in the driveway backed out. She backed out letting the garage door down by remote control as she drove away. Two cars returned to their original positions in the driveway. The four drivers came back into the house, made themselves comfortable on the sofa facing the dining room table. All the men behind the wall came out. They broke up in pairs of two's and began searching through room after room. All the rooms were being searched except for the kitchen and dining room. Sgt. Jerone turned toward me. He looked me straight into my eyes as he began by saying, "You're in a lot of trouble. Do you realize it?" He pulled out some papers. Pushed them in front of me. I didn't look at them. I asked him to get me some orange juice from the refrigerator. He got up and went into the kitchen. I told him where he could find a glass and the juice. He got the glass, filled it with juice and placed it in front of me. I drank the whole glass straight down. While placing the glass on the table, I looked down at the paper. Sgt. Jerone told me to read and sign it. I did so. I pushed the paper over to him.

"I guess that's the end of my job," I said.

"What time do you go to work?" He asked.

"I have to be there at 11:30 a.m."

"We'll see that you get there on time. This paper says you have the right to remain silent. You have the right to an attorney. Do you understand? Do you want to tell us all about it? We already know more than you think we do. The man who was here earlier with the gray car works with us. We already have what you gave to him. So you know that you don't have any way out. You can make it easy on yourself by telling us all you know and who else is in with you. Let me remind you there are certain things we already know. So if I catch you in a lie, I'm going to throw every charge I can at you. On the other hand, if you cooperate, we will do all we can to make things light on you."

"How do I know I can trust you?"

"Look. I'm not on anyone's side. I'm doing my job. What you did is causing me to be here. If I wasn't a fair person, I wouldn't have given it a second through about breaking your door in. So how about it?"

"O.K. I'll tell you. I think it's better to start from the beginning."

"Fine with me. Go."

CHAPTER THREE

Three years ago, I had a fairly good job working for the state in the engineering field. It wasn't enough money to take care of the family needs, but we stretched it. It paid the bills. One day in September, I received notice that all temporary employees were to be laid off due to lack of state funding. Five hundred, twenty-five people, including myself was sent to the unemployment line.

For weeks I went from one job lead to another. I traveled from central state to northern state to southern state. I received a lot of promises, but no job. I read the newspaper, followed friends' leads, and often went to employment agencies. One day, I happened to be reading an article of current events. Under the article was a small advertisement asking for people to apply for the Correction Officer's test. I sat for a few minutes thinking about the job. "No." I said to myself. That's not my kind of work.

Two days later, I was turned down for a job I thought was in the bag. My funds at that point were almost on "E." My wife had started worrying about where the next dollar was coming from. I thought about the prison job again. This time I decided it wouldn't hurt to at least take the test. If I passed and still didn't have a job by the time I got certified, I might consider it.

Three weeks later I took the test. Two weeks after that I received notice to appear at the prison for a job interview. Jane was happy that the prison called me in. She said she knew I would get the job.

The next morning I got up early, drove to the prison. When I arrived, I had to park on the street because part of the new parking lot was blocked off. Construction was in progress everywhere. The prison was a massive structure three stores tall. One complete rectangular block. Present inmate population nearing two thousand. An addition construction for at least a thousand more cells was nearly completed. I walked around to different sides of the prison without finding the entrance. A guard happened to be walking around the structure. I stopped him for directions. He pointed to a narrow cat walk.

I walked through the double set of doors. Inside, I found myself standing on a large square filled with chairs and a walkway going completely around them. There were three levels of different activities going on. On the ground level, there were several entrances going into the inmate's area. A mail and package drop off room was directly opposite the entrance. There were offices spread along the walls. There was an elevator which ran up and down the three levels. The second and third levels had three foot glass railings covering three sides. All the partitions were made of glass. I could see various people working. The third level looked like it was reserved for upper management. On the second was the Personnel Office.

I caught the elevator and went to the second level where I got off and went to the receptionist's desk. I told her why I was here. She directed me to an area, saying that someone would be over to see me shortly. In the meantime, she wanted me to fill out some forms. Just as I finishing, a man walked over to me. He introduced himself. Then took my papers and read them silently.

"You know how to bake?" He asked.

"Yes," I replied. "I have been baking off and on for over ten years."

"Good. We are looking for a baker. Let me get in contact with our food service supervisor."

"O.K., but that's not the job I was applying for."

"Talk with her anyway."

I sat waiting. About twenty minutes later, a short, stocky, half-gray-haired lady in her forties get off the elevator. She walked over to me. "Are you the baker?" She asked.

"Yes, but I'm not applying for that job," I said.

"Maybe I can convince you into taking this job. This job does not require nights. No double back-to-back work shifts." She went on for about twenty minutes explaining what I would be doing, my working hours and special things she was planning with the use of a baker. "Let me take you into see the bakery work area."

I left all my papers with the receptionist.

We rode the elevator down to the first level. I followed her to one of the entrances leading into the prisoner's population area. A guard stood at the entrance. He asked me to empty out all of my pockets and walk through a metal detector. I did so. He patted my body in search for any items that the metal detector didn't pick up as contraband to be taken inside the prison. Next, he checked the contents that came from my pockets. I passed. He told me to pick up my items and move to one side. The lady did the same except instead of patting her down, he waved a metal detector close to her body. It went off near her waist. She was asked to take off her belt. He waved it over her again. This time she passed. He let us in. She led the way.

We walked through nine doors, which were all locked. A "Press" button was provided for each door with a sign written, PRESS TO OPEN. When she did, I could hear the lock click as the metal door opened. After entering the last of the nine doors, a Correction Officer was sitting in a booth on the other side. He watched us as we walked out of sight. No one said a word. When we finally reached our destination, we were standing in a circular room known as the Center. There were ten doors leading into this Center coming from mostly cell block areas. In the middle there was a walk-through metal detector. All inmates were required to pass through when entering the Center. Directly across from where we entered was a depressed area partly thick cage front. We walked around the detector, down a set of steps and waited at a cage door until an officer came with a key. He let us in. This was the dining area. It was larger than a basketball court. Six inmates were cleaning the floor and tables. In the middle of this dining area sat a man in plain clothes with two inmates. He was explaining to them their duties. One inmate was listening while the other was eating ice cream.

"This is Mr. Wilson," said the lady as A.B. and I shook hands without him standing. "Show him around the cookhouse." She directed A.B.

A.B. rose from his seat. He showed me the complete operation in basic form. Just these were mentioned about all the cooks jobs and working areas. He asked, "What do you think about the job?"

"It sounds better all the time. I do think I would like this more than just standing all the time and watching inmates."

"I'll tell my boss you are interested in the job. Let me get you an escort back to where you came in. Someone should give you a call in about a week. If you don't hear from anyone by that time, give us a call."

I shook his hand again. He called a cook to escort me back to where I came in.

Ten days passed. I had not received any word. I decided to give them a call. The institution said they had been trying for three days to get in contact with me. I was told to be there tomorrow at 10 a.m. When Jane came home from work, I told her. She as delighted.

The next morning when I arrived, I checked in with the receptionist. I filled out more forms. They took my picture and gave to me an identification card. I was finger printed. And at the Nurse's Office I had to take a basic physical plus give some blood for testing. After that I was told to report for work tomorrow morning at 6 a.m.

CHAPTER FOUR

The next morning, I reported to the prison. I followed the direction through the nine doors that the lady had shown me. When I arrived at the cookhouse, one of the cooks pointed me in the direction of A.B.'s office. I entered his office to find him sitting at a small desk reading a newspaper. He stopped to look up at me and asked if I was ready to go to work.

I replied "Yes. Do you have a menu for me?"

"There's four inmates working in the bakery. They have a menu. Let's go to the bakery."

The bakery was dirty. It needed painting in the worst way. As I looked around, I could see paint peeling from the ceiling and walls and I could see someone had dumped loose bread in piles on empty bread racks. Some of it had spilled onto the floor. Racks filled with bread stacked fifteen-high were everywhere. Other ingredients were stacked on pallets along one wall. One inmate was lying on a pallet stack of flour sleeping. A.B. woke him up. He told him if he ever caught him lying on the ingredients again, he was going to fire him. The other three inmates were making cookies with an ice cream scoop. They laughed knowing that if the inmates was to get fired, he'd be back in the bakery a couple weeks later.

"This will be where you will spend most of your time," he said.

"That's Ratless with the ice cream scoop. This is Buck. The inmate mashing down the dough is Dick. And that's Ben by the door. They're all yours. Guys, this is Mr. Wilson. Don't be giving him any bull."

I talked to the men for about 30 minutes while they worked. I went into how we were going to make better products, keep the bakery cleaner and what I was expecting from them.

For the next six months, we worked and made improvements. More inmates were coming to eat because of the deserts. One day I was sitting in the bakery alone, working on a recipe. Someone quietly came into the bakery. He closed the steel cage door behind him. I looked up to see who it was. It was Ben. I went back to writing. He came over to me and flashed six one-hundred dollar bills in front of me.

"How would you like to have this in your pocket?" He said.

"No, I don't think so. I make pretty good money as it is," I replied.

"We could be partners. I can show you how to make a lot more to add to what you're now making."

"No! Put your money away." I went back to working on the recipe.

"Don't say no. Think about it. I got plenty of contacts."

I continued to show no interest. Without further words, he slowly walked away and disappeared the same way he entered the bakery.

A week later as I entered the bakery, I smelled the scent of marijuana in the air. I walked in to find three inmates standing behind a couple stacks of bread with their hands behind them. One of them produced a lit joint.

"Do you want a hit?" He asked.

"No. I'm not into that."

He smiled. "Everybody's into smoking weed."

"I don't. Anyway, how can you smoke that stuff at breakfast time?"

"Easy." He said. Then started laughing. The other two joined in on the laughter. I told them they had to go or I would report them. They left.

Over the course of several months, Ben had done everything he could to get in tight with me. He was a great worker. He would do any job I asked. He even volunteered to do extra. One day he came to me with a problem.

"I know I told you several times in the past that my mother was very sick. When her health permits, she brings me packages on visits. But lately, she has been too sick to come. There are some things I have been trying to get her to bring to me. I have no other relatives in the area. I was wondering if you could go to her house to get them for me if I set up a visit between you and her."

"Let me think about it."

"She only lives fifty miles from here. It wouldn't take you any more then about two-and-a-half hours, round trip. Just to show you I'm not trying to take advantage of you, I'll give you a hundred bucks. Think about it. I really need that package."

I watched him as he walked away.

The next day after we had finished working, everyone had left the bakery except Ratless. I was taking a bread inventory when he walked up to me. He pulled out a small flat bag containing some greenish brown substance resembling marijuana.

"Do you know how much this cost in here?"

"No. And I'm not interested in knowing."

"Listen. Don't get bent out of shape. This little pack cost $25 in here. It's equal to two-thirds of a nickel bag. The person controlling the supply of this could clean up. It wouldn't be any risk. Nobody would know who the supplier is. I could buy you all the protection you need inside here and outside the prison. We could set up a deal. I would pay you cash, either in here or when you pick up the package. When I was in another jail, this guard used to bring it in for me every week. He didn't have any problems. Visitors supplied the inmates with cash."

"How was that possible?"

"Visiting females would wrap up the money in single bills in plastic real tight, put it in their mouth before entering the jail. When she kissed the inmate, she would use her tongue to push the wrapped bill into his mouth. He would swallow it. Within twenty-four hours, it would pass through his system. The money would be cleaned up and ready to spend."

"What happened to the guard and why did you stop dealing with him?"

"He got greedy. He wanted more money, plus he was giving me light bags. I wasn't making anything anymore. So I told him to forget it. Right now, this prison is a floating bank. Almost every inmate has money to spend one way or another. Look at this," He went behind a stack of bread racks. A minute later he returned with ten one hundred-dollar bills in his hand. "Check this out. This ain't nothing. This could be one day's business."

"The game and show looks and sounds good, but I can't get into this."

"This ain't no game. I wish I could convince you that I could sell a whole pound of weed in one day. The demand outweighs the supply. You should know about that theory. Just look at the money you could be making. Easy money that would make your pay check look sick."

"I don't want to talk about it anymore."

"O.K., but think about what I said." He went back behind the bread stacks. In just a few minutes he returned and left the area. I finished up my work for the day, signed out and left for home.

The next afternoon, Ben came back for his answer about the package.

"I don't know," I said. "I think I can get in trouble. I understand that I'm not allowed to do things for inmates."

"Hey man. It's only food and clothes. If you go pick it up, I'm gonna pay you. It ain't like I'm trying to use you. You can even give the package to someone else to bring in here for you. I'll give you money for them, too."

"What's so special about this package?"

"I need the clothes. The food, I can do without. But it's something I want."

"O.K. I'll get it for you, but if it starts to cause me problems, I'm gonna let it go. What's the address?"

"Call this number first." He wrote a phone number on a piece of paper. "Make sure she's there before you go. Here's the address. Call around 7 p.m. this evening. I'll call before you call so she'll know whose calling."

"Who do I ask for?"

"Ask for Brenda. Here's $150 for going."

"That cool. If she's there, your package will be picked up this evening. I can't promise you, you'll get it tomorrow, but it will be delivered here by the following day."

I put the money and address in my pocket.

"Solid," he said and walked away.

CHAPTER FIVE

I called Brenda around 7 p.m. that evening. She said Ben had called. The package had been readied for pick up. I told her I would be there within the next two to three hours. She said that would be fine. I hung up.

I was alone at home. Jane was at the beauty salon. Bill and Sam were at her mother's house. I wrote a note saying I had to go out and would be back late tonight. I placed the note on the face of the microwave oven where the mail was usually kept on top. I grabbed my coat and went out the door to my car and drove off for Belville.

The ride took about two hour and twenty minutes. Belville was a small town. Being I had been here before, I had no problem finding Allen Park Place. She lived in a twenty-story apartment building. Her apartment was on the fifteenth floor. I went over to the elevator and press the button. I waited and waited and waited. Ten minutes passed. No elevator. It figures. In a low rent apartment building, most of the time the elevators are out of order.

About that time, an elderly lady came in. "Sonny," she called to me. I turned to face her and I smiled. "The elevator's not working. You got to take the stairs." She pointed toward the stairway. I thanked her and headed toward the steps.

As I walked through the doorway and started walking up the stairs, I stopped on the second landing. I said to myself. If those guys my age can run to the top of the Empire State Building, I should be able to handle these steps. I walked over to the steps leading to the next level, Looking up through the stairs, I thought I would reach heaven before I reached her floor. I started running up the steps, taking them two at a time. On the way up, I passed the lady who spoke to me going upward. When I got to the fifteenth floor, I was out of breath. I checked my watch. I had run up fifteen flights in two minutes. The hallway was silent and long and could use more lighting. I checked the letters on the doors until I found 15K. I rang the bell located in the center, top portion of the door. A nice looking lady in her late forties opened the door walking with an old cane.

Is Brenda home?" I asked.

"Yes she is."

"I'm the person who called over two hours ago."

She invited me in and shut the door behind me. I stood waiting while she went to get the package. She returned with it and handed it to me without further words. She opened the door and I left. Going back down the stairs, I passed the same lady still coming up to the ninth floor. "Have a nice day." I said. She replied with something that I didn't fully understand. When I had arrived at the first floor, there was a man working on the elevator. I said to myself, he would come to fix it while I was leaving. I got into my car and headed for home.

The next morning when I arrived for work, Ben was waiting for me at the bakery entrance. Before I could say anything, he pulled me off to one side.

"Did you get the clothes and food?" He asked.

"Yeah, but I'm not going to bring it inside. I have someone who is willing to take care of it."

He smiled and shown signs of excitement. "Talk to them. See if they can get it here today."

"Look. If I'm going to be bothered about your stuff, I'll give you your money back and I'll take your stuff back."

He started to calm down. "O.K. O.K. I'll wait until tomorrow."

We worked all day without any further conversation pertaining to the package.

That evening I made contact with Sharlene. I told her I wanted her to do something for me tomorrow. It's important that I meet with her this evening. I got the package and rushed to her place. She answered the door on the first ring.

"What's happening?" She said as I walked in. She easily closed the door behind me.

"I got this package I want delivered to the mail and package room at the prison. Can you take it there before noon tomorrow?"

"Yeah, I can drop it off during my travels. Do I need any ID?" Anyway, what's in the package?"

"The package contains clothes and food. There's nothing for you to worry about. No drugs or anything like that. Yes you'll need your I.D. Here's $25 for you. This is how important it is for the receiver. Before I forget, here's his name and prison number." I opened the bag and we lightly looked the contents over to make sure there was no contraband inside. "O.K.?" I asked.

"O.K. Thank for the money."

10:30 a.m.

Sharlene arrived at the prison. She had no problem finding a parking space in the completed parking lot. She entered the building carrying the package. At the mail and package window, she had to stand in line. When her turn came, she placed the package on the window ledge.

"Can I help you?" Said the officer on the other side.

"Yes. I want this package to go to Ben. Here's his last name, number and cell block."

"Do you have any I.D.?"

She took out her wallet. Retrieved two pieces of I.D. and placed them on the ledge. "My Driver's License and work I.D. Will that work?"

"Yeah. Write on this form what's in the package and sign it. We'll x-ray anything we can't open."

"Will he get the package today? It has food in it."

"Yeah. He'll have it by 5 p.m. if everything clears."

Sharlene picked up her cards and left.

I took my two given days off from work. I needed the time to rest. The bakery crew had been working on making pies and cookies earlier that morning on the day I when back to work. I was all charged up ready for work. When I entered the bakery, I could smell the scent of pot in the air. All four bakers were there with three other inmates standing close together. I could sense something wasn't right.

"What's happening guys?" I asked.

"Nothing really," replied Ben. "We finished work and was taking a break."

"Something's got to be up. Seven people in here. Nobody cleaning up?" Ben told the three other inmates, who were not bakers to leave. The other three bakers started working, but became confused as to what they should be doing. I called Ben over to one side. Before I could say a word, he said, "That stuff was out of sight."

"What stuff are you talking about?"

"The food. Those two large bags of potato chips had 15 packages of pot each mixed in with the potato chips. Yeah, the bags were opened and glued back together with Krazy Glue. I just sold to last two packets."

I looked at him in disbelief. In a low voice I said, "I could have gotten in trouble. And that poor girl could have gone to jail. I don't believe you did this to me!"

"Cool down. You're not the only guy bringing stuff in here. The officer working in the Center changes cars every year with the money he's making bringing stuff in here."

"Don't ever ask me to do you another favor ever again. Do you understand?"

"Check this out. I didn't sell all the stuff like I said a minute age. I saved four packets. Don't say a word until I'm done. I figured you might get cold feet and quit on me. I noticed how you are always straightening up those loaves when you take inventory. Well, I use a pair of plastic serving gloves to pick up one of those loaves.

"I dumped all the bread out. Then I put those four packets inside the loaf bags. Your finger prints are on the bag. Do you dig? Not mine. I have the bags hidden where no one can find them except me. So sonny boy, if you don't play ball with me, all I have to do is pass off word that you are bringing pot into the prison. This should open the eyes of the prison investigators. Then for a price, I can pay a stool pigeon to drop a dime to the investigators telling where the bags of pot are with your finger prints on them. Who do you think they are going to believe?" Ben held his hands up in the air.

"This is blackmail," I said.

"No man, this is business. You're going to make some good money and you're going to thank me in the end. So be cool. I'm going to show you how it's done." We worked the rest of the day together. I lost all respect for him.

When I returned home that evening, all I could think about was how am I going to deal with this mess safely and still keep my job. Several thoughts came to mind. I could pay to have him knocked off. But I imagined some of his friends might know about the package. I didn't want his blood on my hands. Then I thought I could just quit my job. But what would I do for income? I could tell the investigators. They would probably have me fired for disobeying the rules. Or I could go along with program. I decided to go along with the program until I can find the best way out.

CHAPTER SIX

The next day after we had finished work, I called Ben to one side.

"What other ways can I get the stuff to you without getting anyone else involved?" I asked.

"So you want to talk?"

"Yeah. I want to know the whole deal."

"O.K. Here's the deal. Go up to the supply room. Get a pair of work boots for yourself. Get them one size larger then you normally wear. So if you wear size 10, get size 11. When you pick up the weed, weigh it up into one-ounce plastic bags. Roll them up, but not too tight. Put two one-ounce bags into another bag. Wrap those up, but not too tight. Tape the packs so they don't come loose. Then take your boots. Loosen all the strings. Next, take six two-ounce packs, if you have that many and place them on the floor. With your bare foot, press down hard on the pack to remove the air. Then take two packs and place them on the inside of your boot. Don't push them all the way up. Behind them on the inside heel, place one more pack. If the pack don't fill up the heel, place a single ounce next to it. O.K. So now you stick your foot into your boot on top of the packs. It might be a little tight at first, but stand on them for a few seconds and they'll go down a little more. The more you walk on the weed, the more it will go down. At a certain thickness it won't go down anymore. O.K. Tighten up the strings. Your feet will feel a little funny at first. But it will look natural.

Every now and then you might have to tighten up the string because the weed will begin to pack. You can carry twelve to fourteen ounces at a time in. Also, you can put one-ounce rolls in your under briefs. One on each side of your nuts in the small of your crotch. The guards won't search in those areas. They are not allowed to. If you do just as I say, you won't ever have any problems. Don't ever panic if they squeeze your ankles. The weed will be below that level. I'll let you know when the next pickup is going to be ready."

"O.K. How much am I going to be paid per trip?"

"You'll be paid $150 per stop, either by me or when you get there. If you make three stops, you got $450 coming. O.K.?"

"I can live with that for one night's travel."

"We'll talk about it some more when I set up your next trip."

The next week Ben set me up for a trip. This time it was to his brother's location. He gave me the phone number for whom to call, whom I was to talk with, the time to call and complete address. I asked for my money in advance. He went out of the bakery. Ten minutes later he returned with the cash.

"You'll be picking up twelve ounces." He said. "This means you should be able to bring it all in at one time."

That evening, as I sat at my dinner table eating, I said to Jane, "I have to go out around 8 p.m. I might not be back until 2 or 3 a.m."

She looked at me funny like. "You were out late last week. What's so important for you to stay out that late? When you're here, you can't wait to go to bed at 10 p.m. I have been asking you to stay up with me. No, but now you're starting to go out at night."

"Cool it. It's strictly business." At that point, she didn't say another word.

8:00 p.m.

I made the phone call to Funbun. I still didn't know how to get there even with the instructions given to me. I went to my car. Instead of going back into the house, I stayed in my car looking up the town on my map. There it was. 36 miles south of here. I set out on my trip.

Funbun was a small town. I went straight through it without even seeing the name on any signs. When I finally realized it, I was at a sign saying 'Funbun 7 miles' in the opposite direction. I drove back the seven miles. At a telephone booth, I made another call to the location I was to go. Ben's brother picked up the phone and told me to stay where I was. He would come pick me up in about five minutes.

A small store was next to the phone booth. I went in and bought a large bag of popcorn. I came back out to wait for Ben's brother beside by my car. I had just started to eat my popcorn when a dark blue, late model BMW pulled up. I recognized the car through the phone call description. He waved for me to follow him. I got into my car, placed the bag of popcorn onto the passenger's seat. I followed him to a location off the main road for about a quarter mile. We parked next on the grass in the front yard. Then walked together toward a house. He asked me some questions about Ben. I responded, but he wasn't interested in a long conversation about him. We entered the house. He offered me a seat. I sat and looked around when all of a sudden there was a knock at the door. Then the person knocking called out "Tim?" Tim responded by saying, "Come in. The door's open." Four guys came in. All looking like they were high.

"I'm not holding right now," said Tim. "Why don't all of you wait here for about fifteen minutes while I make a run. That includes you too." He was referring to me with the point of his finger.

"O.K." we all agreed.

We waited. The four guys talked among themselves, laughing and horsing around. Tim returned. He gave me my package. Half of the job was over. I was on my way back toward home.

About thirteen miles outside of Funbun, a patrol car pulled out of nowhere. He turned on his flashing lights as he pulled up behind me. While slowing down to a stop, I pushed the package under my seat. I became slightly nervous. I wondered if Tim had set me up. I also thought a lot of things while I sat waiting for the officer to get out of his vehicle. I tried pushing the package further under my seat but it was as far back as it could go. I sat up straight. Suddenly I heard the vehicle door slam. He walked up to my vehicle. I rolled down the window.

"Let me see your license and registration."

While I was digging them from my wallet, he turned on his flash light. First he shined it in the back. Then in the front and finally, the light came to rest on my bag of popcorn. I handed him the papers. He shined the light on the papers.

"Do you know you were going ten miles over the speed limit?"

"No sir. I didn't see any signs pertaining to the speed limit along the road."

He shined the light back onto the popcorn bag. "What's in the bag?" He asked.

"Popcorn."

"Hand it over. Let me see."

I gave him the bag. He took the popcorn bag out of a bag. Looked inside the empty bag. Placed the popcorn back inside and handed it back to me.

"I'm going to give you a warning this time. Slow down." He gave me back my paper after giving me the warning. I continued on my way home with my heart racing.

The next morning I got up early before anyone in the house woke up. I weighed all the weed like Ben had told me. I used a pound scale that I had for several years. I managed to get my feet into the boot. The weed felt lumpy under pressure. At first it didn't fit right. But after several tries, I was about to get my feet in a good position. I felt like I was on stilts. By the time I got my feet adjusted, it was time to report for work. Still no one had awakened. I let without making a sound.

When I arrived, the officers were changing shifts. This meant I wouldn't have any problem getting in. The officers were moving quickly through the metal detector and shake down. I got in line. My turn came. I placed everything in my pockets on a bench like table. Then walked through the metal detector. No alarm sounded. The officer ran his hands across my chest, around my waist and down each trouser leg to meet the top of my socks. While he was running his hands down the sides of my legs, I began to feel a little nervous. But then, he told me to pick up my stuff and move inside. I had made it in. clear and home free. My only problem now would be to make sure no one sees me with the weed or passing it off.

I walked the distance to the bakery. When I arrived, all the bakers were working. I went in. Ben looked at me waiting for a sign that I had made the connection. I nodded to let him know that I had it on me. I told the other three bakers to go into the basement and bring up twenty cases of sliced peaches for tonight's desert. As soon as they left, I blocked the gate door so no one could enter the bakery. I took Ben to the back of the bakery so if anyone was passing by the doorway, they would not see us. We stood behind several bread racks. I emptied my boots. The weed was transferred to his boots. The other two rolls in my under briefs, I took them out and passed them off to him. He in turn, put them down into the front of his trousers.

"That's how it's done," said Ben.

I stayed in the bakery. Ben went out into the dining area. There he passed off all twelve bags. He returned while the other three bakers were bringing up cases of fruit. He joined in.

As I worked an idea came to me. Ratless is interested in the same thing. Why don't I put him in competition with Ben. Ratless would get the taste of money and would do anything for it. He could slow Ben down and help dry up the prison's cash. Ben couldn't hold anything on me if he tried to set me up for a bust. That would put Ratless out of business. Ratless would have him bumped off. I decided to do just that.

I got Ratless alone in the back of the bakery after all the inmates had left. "Do you remember talking to me about making some money?" I asked.

"Yeah."

"Well, I have considered taking you up on it." The way he looked at me, you would have thought I told him he was free to leave the prison.

"Hey man," he said. "This is the best move you could ever make. We're gonna do good. I'll get in contact with my people this evening and see how fast I can get things rolling."

"Hold it. We ain't finished talking just yet. I want $150 for each trip. And I want it before you get yours or I'm going to hold up your package."

"O.K. You'll get your money when you pick up the package."

"I don't want any bull crap, O.K.?"

"O.K."

Ratless got his people together. I started making runs all over the state for him. Most of his people met me in odd places like gas stations, corners and beaches. Between Ben and Ratless, I stayed on the road four nights a week. I never told Jane the full story of what I was doing. All she knew was that I was working with some guy doing some special job to increase our income. As long as she saw the extra money, she didn't question what I was doing.

CHAPTER
SEVEN

Drugs started pouring into the prison more rapidly than ever. Almost every inmate was spending cash on his favorite drug. The yard became a market place, and a testing ground. Inmate dealers were advertising their drugs to be the best all over the prison. They even thought up new names to give drugs in an effort to increase sales.

The money started drying up faster than the dealers expected. The amount of weekly visitors started trailing off. Visiting the prison was no longer a matter of visiting inmates. It became a money transferring Activity. Inmates who didn't receive visits would trade off store supplies, personal clothing and cigarettes. When inmates ran out of things to give for drugs, credit came into existence. Friends of drugs dealers would write home to ask friends and relatives to send checks to people they were indebted to. The checks didn't always show up on time. Sometimes the checks didn't come at all. Dealers couldn't wait weeks or months for monies they needed to buy more drugs. Therefore, these inmates had to resort to having money taken from their prison accounts. Tempers flared. Contracts were put out on delinquent payers. Inmates with serious debt problems would not go to the yard. By now, the yard had also become a battle ground. Better known as a war zone. Fights and stabbings were becoming an almost everyday thing. The war over drugs had gotten so bad that stool pigeons were dropping notes to

Internal Affairs to put dealers out of business in an effort to get them off their back. A fight broke out in the yard where two inmates had large debts that they could not pay because all of their funds had dried up and their connections on the outside refused to send them funds which ended causing them to be shanked by several inmates where one died on the scene and the other needed medical attention that was supplied by the prison. Word never reached the streets because the incident was confined behind prison walls.

Correction officers were often caught up in yard fights. They had resorted to wearing special gear to protect themselves from harm during their watch in the yard.

The accounting section for inmates' funds, which once processed checks on a daily basis, now had a six-week back up. Often the accounting section found itself under pressure from the inmates' committee.

Sally was a long-time employee of the prison. She was the only person who took care of inmates' accounts. Her desk was located on the open secretarial section on the second level near her boss's office. On this particular day, she had gotten fed up with her work load. She walked into her supervisor's office. "Boss," she said. "My pile of accounts to be processed are getting larger every week. When am I going to get some help? I can't continue to work like this. There's a lot of pressure on me for these accounts to be processed. And not to mention my other work."

"Sally," he paused for a minute. "You know our budget is limited. If I could get you someone, I would. I'll tell you what I'll do. I'll let you work an extra two hours three days a week until you catch up. How does that sound?"

"That's not going to get it. I can't work overtime because then I'd have to pay my baby sitter extra for keeping my kids later."

"Well, I'm sorry I can't bail you out right just this minutes. But I'll talk with the Warden to see what can be done. O.K.?"

CHARLES FEGGANS

"I'm telling you, Boss, I don't like it. But I'll give you a few days before I check with you again." Sally went back to her deck. Boss sat thinking. Suddenly, he rose from his seat and went to Warden Tony's office.

Warren Tony started with the prison system some 32 years ago as an accounting clerk. Through the years, he worked his way up to become the Warden.

When the Supervisor entered Warden Tony's officer, Tony was sitting behind his desk reading from a stack of papers on his desk. "Have a seat," said Warden Tony. "What's the problem?"

"How do you know I have a problem?"

"You never come to my office without something on your mind. I'm I right?"

"Sort of. Any way. It's the inmates' accounts. All of a sudden we are over loaded with check requests. Most of these request are for cash transfers from one inmate to another. I think the situation deserves looking into."

"Warden Tony picked up his telephone. He dialed some numbers. "Hello. May I speak with Henry?" There was a short silence. Then abruptly he spoke out. "Hi Henry. This is Warden Tony. Can you come up to my office immediately?" Another silence. Then, "Thanks."

Warden Tony and the supervisor were talking when Henry entered the room. Henry was one of the Internal Affairs investigators. His job was to put down disturbances that put the prison in an uproar.

"Henry," said Warden Tony, "Can you find out why there are as many check request going to the inmates' accounting section?" Henry gave a yes gestor with the nod of his head. "Whatever you come up with, I would like a verbal report as soon as possible."

"Right now," said Henry. "I think we have a pretty good idea of who is behind this problem. I just needs a little more time to investigate."

"Tell me more."

"I don't know if you are aware of the fact that there's a drug war going on. We have been keeping an eye on some of the dealers though information provided by informers. But we can't catch them carrying anything or find stuff in their cell. An as to who is bringing in the stuff, we don't have any leads at all.

"Supervisor," said Warren Tony. "Let's try a long shot. I'm going to give you four officers. I want you to have one of your people work with them. I want them to go through all the cash request slips for the past six months. Separate them into piles so we can see who they are sending money to. This way we can see who is receiving this money and in what amounts."

"Sounds like a good idea," said the Supervisor. "How soon will you give me the officers?"

"I'll set it up starting tomorrow if it's O.K. with you."

"Tomorrow will be fine."

The Supervisor and Henry left Warden Tony's office. When the supervisor returned to his area, he called Sally in. He told her about the idea Warden Tony had suggested.

"I'll work with the officer," said Sally.

Henry went straight to the tower overlooking the inmates in the yard. He climbed up a high ladder to get to where he wanted to go. And when he reached the top, he could see the yard in full view. The yard was the size of two football fields placed side by side. The officer in the tower allowed Henry to borrow his binoculars to see across to the other side. Three-quarters of the way across the field, he could see a small group of inmates standing around Ratless. They appeared to be passing something that looked like a cigarette. He knew Ratless was a dealer through his informers but as of yet was unable to catch him with anything on him. Henry watched until the yard was called in. He used the tower's phone to call the center.

"Who am I speaking with?" Asked Henry. "Who? O.K. I want inmate Ratless pulled over to the side when he comes in from the yard.

I'm going to need an officer to go with us when I take him away." He hung the phone up.

In single file, the inmates walked from the yard into the building. Guards standing outside their towers watched with a watchful eye. They held their shotguns pointing straight up in the air. As the inmates entered, the guards in the Center were giving them instructions to correct things they were doing that was wrong. The line going through the detector was long. They were required to take off all metals such as watches, chains and belt buckles. On the other side of the detector, officers were standing by gates leading to cell blocks. The inmates talked and joked as they walked along.

Rarless entered the building. Immediately an officer called him to one side.

In an angry voice, Rarless called out. "What did I do now? You guys are always messing with me."

"Be quiet!" Said the officer.

Henry came in. He told the officer to follow him and bring Ratless along. They walked through several doors to a small room. Henry opened the door. He told the officer to wait outside. Ratless went inside. Henry followed him. Henry took a seat on one side of the table while he told Ratless to be seated on the other side.

"You got a pretty good thing going don't you? I was watching you today while you were in the yard. I saw you and a few other guys passing around a joint."

"Man, this is jail. Where would I get weed from? You know you can't grow anything out there in that yard."

"You know what I'm talking about. I know you've been selling stuff in the yard. Informers have been telling me you've been putting contracts out on people. Come clean. You don't have to give me that bull crap. I saw your record. You serving twenty-five years for armed robbery."

"That's what my record says. I didn't do it."

"Yeah. That's what they all say. I got a deal for you. You've been in here for almost ten years. That means you got fifteen more to go. What if I tell you I can get you out of here in two more years if you give us names of your suppliers? It has to be someone bringing drugs in from the outside. And it has to be proven."

Ratless had to think about it for a few minutes. "Is this really on the up and up?"

"If you'll agree. I'll get it in writing for you and have it put into your record. The situation is really getting bad. You know it for yourself."

"All right. Bring me back some papers, then I'll give you all the information I know."

CHAPTER EIGHT

By now, I had traveled around the state so much, I had the felting I could go anywhere without a map. Many of the people I met were not all dealers. But quite a few were. Some became my friends. After all, we had interest in the drug business. Some of those dealers had friends who were also dealing in other drugs. I met and became friends with some of them as well. They were rolling in money. I remembered this one guy whose family had a weed factory in Florida. He use to always tell me. "I can see you like to travel. I can show you how to make some real money. I don't know why you keep fooling around with petty change. If I could get you to make one trip to Florida, I'd fatten your pocket with about thirty-five G's".

"The money sounds good," I would replied. "But it's just too many cops between here and there. My luck of getting through is not good. I'd get stopped for something either dumb or stupid." He would laugh. I would change the subject or just walk away.

Now that I had more money to burn, I would treat my family to expensive meals, buy them things they had been wishing to have and putting a little away for that rainy day. Life was treating me well. However, my wife started worrying about me. I would never tell her what my business was all about, but I would assure her that, no matter what I was doing, I wasn't running around on her. Every time I gave her an extra $100, she would dismiss the thoughts until she had spent the money.

I continued to work at the prison. I had been transporting weed so long, I didn't get nervous anymore. Half the time, the guards didn't pat me down. In fact, I was one of the last persons to be suspected. Now that things were going well, I would even leave during the day to pick up weed from my home to bring back during working hours. I would do this when I picked up over a pound that had to be delivered on certain days.

It had been raining for the last two days. I had picked up a two pound package for Ben. I brought one pound in to work with me. Ben had been waiting for me in the bakery. As I walked in, he asked? "Hey. What's happening?"

"You know."

"All right. My man's waiting for the stuff. How much did you bring in?"

"For now. I have just one pound."

"I got to have both of them today. Can you get the other one in this morning?"

"I don't know. It's still raining out. My car went into a slide last night because of the wet road and half-bald tires. It might not be safe for me to make another trip."

"Look man. You don't understand. I need it. This guy's got the bucks. I can't let another dealer get to him."

"O.K. I'll go for it. But it'll have to be about three hours from now. I got things to do up until then."

"I can wait that long. But it's got to be before noon."

I gave him the pound I was holding after he had locked the gate. Just after we completed the transfer, the other bakers came to work. Ben left. We started working on the day's products.

9:30 a.m.

It was time for me to make my move. I informed Ben that if anyone was looking for me, I had gone to the other side of the prison to check on pastry supplies. He agreed. I give the other inmates instructions on what to do until I returned.

I made certain not to arouse any unnecessary attention. Before I drove out of the parking lot, I looked around to see if anyone was watching me. Instead of driving through the front gate like I normally do, I decided it was to my best interest to drive through the back gate.

It had stopped raining. The streets were still wet and partly covered with wet leaves. I made it home in about twenty-five minutes. The weed had been bagged up earlier in the morning while everyone in the home slept. As I made my entrance into the house, it was completely silent. My wife was at work. The kids were in school. I loaded the weed into my boots and briefs. I got back into my car and headed toward the prison. As I drove along, I heard the time being given over the radio "Darn," I said to myself. "I've been gone almost an hour. I wonder if I've been missed."

I decided to speed up a little. As I rounded the curve, I saw this oil truck pulling out of a right side street. It was crossing my path on a left-turning angle to face me on the opposite side of the street. I applied my breaks. The car went into a skid. The back started spinning around. The oil truck cleared my path, but the back end continued to spin. BAM! CLINK! CLINK! I had slammed the back end of my car into the truck. The force of the impact forced my car back across the street to rest next to the curve.

The truck stopped. We both got out. I noticed the truck wasn't damaged. Then I looked at my vehicle. The rear bumper had been knocked completely off. The driver walked away saying he was going to call the police. I began to get nervous. Here I was supposed to be at work. I got a pound of weed on me. And now this guy was going to call the police. I decided to stay and play it cool.

I opened the trunk of my vehicle. With my own strength, I picked up the bumper and pushed it inside. It slid all the way toward the back seat. I slammed the trunk shut. Twenty minutes later, the police arrived. We both got into the police car. We gave our identification papers. The officer asked a few questions. He wrote down all the necessary information. No ticket was given to either of us because the accident resulted from a bad weather condition. We were given back our papers and told to consult our insurance companies.

I drove back to the prison thinking I had been missed by now. I drove through the back gate of the parking lot. This time I parked as far away from the building as possible in an effort not to be noticed. I walked to the prison entrance, being careful to keep close to the building so I was out of sight of anyone who might be looking out the second and third level windows. I walked through the double doors and into the lobby. Of all the people in the lobby, Henry from Internal Affairs was standing, talking with a correction officer. I took a glance at him. He was following me with his eyes. I begin to get nervous all over again. This was not my day. I went to the entrance. Henry turned his back to me as he went back to talking with the correction officer.

With everything out of my pockets, I passed through the metal detector. I turned to noticed Henry was standing alone and again watching me. I said nothing as I waited for the go sign. The officer told me to go inside. As I pulled the door open, I heard Henry saying, "Hold it right there." I could feel the blood rush to my head as I turned toward his direction. At that point, I realized he was talking to someone else. I quickly went in and made my way toward the cookhouse.

A.B. spotted me entering the cookhouse. "Hey Wilson," he called out in an angered voice. "Where the hell you been? I've been looking for you for over an hour."

"Didn't the inmates in the bakery tell you I went to the other side to check on their pastry?"

"Yeah. I sent someone over there looking for you. They couldn't find you. Next time you leave here, check with me first. Do you understand that?"

"Yeah."

I went into the bakery. Ben was gone. I locked the gate behind me as I entered. All the weed I had on me, I unloaded it in a bread rack and piled loaves of bread over it. A wave of relief came over me. I had had it for today with everything. Now to get back in good grace with A.B. might be a problem. It was lunch time by now. I went to the serving line to help supervise the serving. Supervising the serving of food was always a problem. Inmates behind the line would often making deals with other inmates coming through the line in the form of giving extra food for store items or cigarettes.

Ben was still in the cookhouse. He was serving on the serving line. I saw an inmate standing around doing nothing. I told him to relieve Ben because he was needed in the bakery. Ben was angry when he approached me.

"Man. I needed this stuff an hour ago." He said.

"Look, if you had to go through the hell I just went through, you would say to hell with this. I just wrecked my car along with having to deal with the street police."

Ben said nothing. I took him to where the weed was in the bakery. It was now his. I left him with it while I returned to the serving area.

The inmate who Ben was supposed to give the weed to had gone. So Ben had to find another spot to hide it until a new buyer came along. Unable to do so, he decided to take it to his cell. This way he might be able to pass it off this evening. If he were to leave it in the bakery, he wouldn't be allowed to enter the bakery during his off shift.

Ben got in the middle of a bunch of inmates leaving the dining area. He laughed and joked with them as they walked along. The metal detector in the center wasn't working. Two outside contractors were working on it. Ben was allowed to walk through it with the switch off. The gate to his cell block opened. He and the rest of the inmates went through and into their cell. An officer came behind them to lock their door from the outside. Ben sat on his bed for a while before deciding whether or not to turn on his television. Suddenly, he leaned back on his bed to get comfortable. There was a rumbling sound on his cell door. He watched as the door opened. There were four officers starring him in the face.

"Ben!" One of the officers called out. "This is a shake down. We want you to come out here in the hallway. Everyone in this cell block is locked in. We're searching each cell. It's your turn."

Ben began to get nervous. There was nothing he could do. He still had the pound on him. He slowly removed himself from the bed. Made his way to the door opening and passed into the hallway. Three of the officers went into his cell. The other officer stayed close to Ben. They look through everything in the cell that could be opened or turned over. Ben was hoping they wouldn't search him. The three officers, not able to find anything, left the cell.

"O.K." Said one of the officers. "You can go back inside." As he did so, the door began to shut behind him. Suddenly, the door stopped and did a reverse. All four officers entered his cell. "We want you to strip down." Said the same officer.

With his face expressionless, he began to remove his clothing.

"Do I have to take off my shoes, too?"

"Yeah. Everything."

"The floor is cold and I don't like standing on it bare foot."

"You should have thought about that before you decided to come to prison."

He realized that this was it for him. He got down on one knee. Slowly he began to unfasten his shoe. Three of the officers were standing beside him watching. When he removed the first shoe, one of the officers took it. His eyes lit up as he began pulling out the bags.

"Well, well, well. Look what we have here. Let's see the other shoe. Take off all your clothes." The officer waited until Ben was completely nude. They were surprised to see four more bags fall from his underwear. After they collected all the weed in one pile, they made him put all his clothing and shoes back on. He was handcuffed and taken away to solitary confinement. The weed was taken to Internal Affairs.

CHAPTER NINE

Sally and the four officers worked on the cash request slips for almost two weeks. They had compiled a long list of names. There were many slips going to the same names with the same addresses. The list was handed over to the Boss. He in turn gave the list to Annie in personnel with a request to see if any of the names matched any of the employees working here at the prison.

During the next two day, Annie was able to come up with twenty-two identifiable employee names. The list was ready. It was time for Annie to confront the Boss with the list she had prepared. When she approached his office, the door was open. She walked in to fine his sitting behind his desk writing. He looked up as she approached.

"Boss, here's your list. There's several names on this list you might know. However, there is one name that really sticks out."

"What might that name be?"

"It's Wilson. The baker. His address matches the address on the cash request slips. He received over $1,000. There are still more slips waiting to be processed with his address on them."

"Thanks you for this information Annie."

The Boss sat analyzing the list. He wrote down several names that he thought were important. He retrieved the telephone.

"Warden Tony please." There was a short silence. "Warden Tony? This is Boss. Annie just gave me a list of names that I think you should look at." There was a moment of silence. "Okay. I'll bring it up right away."

Boss immediately left his office and proceeded to go to Warden Tony's office. Warden Tony was waiting for him.

"Have a seat," he said.

Boss leaned over the desk while handing the list to him and immediately sat in a chair to the side of Warden Tony's desk.

The Warden looked over the list. "This might be the answer to some of our problems. Let me get Henry up here." He called Henry's office. Henry did not answer the phone, but word was passed around for him to go to Warden Tony's office right away. Henry had just returned from talking with inmate Ben who was still in solitaire confinement. Henry, through talking with Ben knew something about the weed deals and the two of them had started making a deal that would let Ben off the hook if he told how he received the weed. But first, he would have to get the Warden's approval. He entered Warden Tony's office. There he took a seat on the opposite side of Boss. "Henry," said Warden Tony. "We compiled this list of names pertaining to cash request slips. The name that stands out like a star is Wilson. He's received about $1,000 from inmates' accounts. The rest of the names received about $200 or less."

He handed the list to Henry.

"A couple of weeks ago," said Henry. "I saw Wilson coming back to work around noon. He looked a little nervous. The more I watched him, the worse he seemed to get. Then that same day, one of his workers got busted in a shake down with a pound of marijuana. Now you give me this list with his name as top receiver. I think we might have something here."

"You're damn right! We do have something." Shouted Warden Tony in an explosive voice. "What's the best way to get to him?"

Henry was quick to speak up. "I have a plan. I can make a deal with inmate Ben. That's with your permission. Or I can make a deal with inmate Ratless. You see, I spotted Ratless in the yard doing business with a group of inmates. With the aid of a few of my informers, he was identified as a big drug dealer. He also works in the bakery. Between the two of them and the State Police Narcotics Division, we should be able to get something on Wilson. If this fails, we can force him to resign."

"Good idea. But I'm not making any deal with any inmates."

"Warden, this is the quickest way to get on the trail to putting some of these guys out of business. The only people who knows about what's happening is us three."

"I know what you're saying. I can't start making deals with killers and robbers. The public wanted them off the streets and by God, I'm not sending them back to do more harm."

"Warden, don't get me wrong. We are not talking about letting inmates out of prison. I was talking in the sense of putting them in solitaire confinement.

"I might go for that, but nothing more."

Henry and Boss left the Warden's Office without further comments.

Most of the drug dealers had been dealing in drug so long, they started getting lax. They became users as well. The secret identity of their suppliers started slipping out when they placed trust in their best friends. In prison, everyone is a friend of someone who has another friend. It didn't take long before the whole prison knew who the outside suppliers were. The informers found out and passed the word along to Internal Affairs.

For the past three weeks, Henry had received a pile of notes from his informers. By now he had gotten a pretty clear picture of the drug operation.

One evening, Henry went to visit Ben, who was still in solitary confinement. After having a few brief words with the officer assigned to that area, he walked to Ben's cell. The door was made from a solid sheet of steel. Near the top of the door was a peep hole. Henry slid the slide open by pushing it to one side. Looking inside, he saw Ben sleeping in his bed. "Ben, Ben. This is Henry." Ben started moving around. Then he raised his head, paused for a moment. With his fingers, he wiped his eyes open. "Ben. Come to the door. I want to talk with you. I had a talk with Warden Tony about your situation."

Ben came to the door. "What did he have to say?"

"He said no deals. Cut and dry." (I lied). "They're going to make an example out of you to show the others what can happen to inmates who want to go big time in the drug business."

"I didn't think you guys were going for anything. If you had planned on doing something, you wouldn't be taking this long to get back to me."

"There's nothing I can do for you. My office is out of it." With those words, Henry had hope that Ben would come clean and give Henry some information on Wilson in light of making his present situation a little better. But Ben was still holding his grounds. Henry closed the peephole. He made his way out of the unit. The thought of Ratless came back to Henry. *Maybe I should visit him.* He said to himself. Ratless' cell was on the other side of the prison. It took him a good ten minutes to get to the cell block area. After making the trip, Henry thought it would be to his best advantage not to go see Ratless. The inmates would see him talking to Ratless and get ideas about Ratless. On the other hand, if Ratless was called out and taken to a private room, he might be willing to cooperate and not be under the pressure of the other inmates. Henry told one of the two officers to bring Ratless up front to a small room. He did so. Henry waited in the room while Ratless was brought in. Henry was already seated and Ratless took a seat across from him with a table between them.

"Words out that you had Bassheer stabbed in the yard yesterday." Said Henry. "Everybody knows he's in heavy debt with you. He turned himself in to protective custody. And the other inmate died who was shanked also. What do you have to say about that?"

"I don't know anything about that. Nobody in this prison owes me anything. I don't know where you getting that bad info from."

"You don't have to be pulling my leg. My informers don't make up things."

There was a short silence.

Henry looked Ratless straight into his eyes. "I told you before that I was willing to make a deal with you. Check this out. We know that Wilson is bringing in drugs. We also know that Wilson is supplying you with weed. We know that Wilson will go anywhere you send him for a price. Do I have to go on?"

"No. I get your drift."

"Now, we want you to send Wilson to pick up a package from one of our men."

"How will I go about that?"

"In a couple of days, we'll provide you with all the necessary information."

"What are you guys going to do for me?"

"We know you're a drug dealer. We want you to continue to operate in the same fashion. If you mess up and get caught, you'll be put in protective custody until we get our man. After Wilson has been nailed, you are to cease all drug sales. No charges are to be filed against you. All other drug dealers will be picked up and prosecuted. We have all their names. Also, you will be transferred to another prison to prevent any retaliation against you."

"If I agree to this, how will I know that word won't spread to the other prison about what's going down?"

"We gonna send you out west where no one will ever know anything about you."

"You got yourself a deal. I agree to this."

Henry called for the officer to return Ratless to his cell.

The next morning I arrived at work a little late. All the bakers were working. We had gotten a replacement for Ben since he was removed from population. I felt a little more at ease. He wouldn't have time now to bust me because he had problems of his own.

Ratless came over to me. "Did you hear the news about Ben?"

"Nothing since he got busted."

"Last night he hung up."

"He what?" I asked in a surprising way. "How did he manage that?"

"He tied one of the sheets around his neck. Got up on the end of his bed. Tied the other end around the bars on the overhead vent. Then jumped. A lot of inmates got out of debt overnight. I know you were supplying him with weed. He told a lot of inmates."

This was not a real surprise to me. An inmate had pulled me off to one side about a month ago to tell me word was out about me bringing in drugs for certain inmates.

"How do we stand?" I asked.

"We cool. I'm making money. You making money. No problems. We in this together. I'm not blowing my game. I'll be making more money since Ben knocked himself out of the picture.

"Good. I just wanted to hear you say that."

"In a couple of days, I got a pick up for you. When I get it hooked up, I'll give you all the info."

"Sure. O.K. Now let's get to work."

During the day, a couple of inmates approached me. They were telling me what had happened to Ben. They also had a game to run down on me about how we could make lots of money. They wanted to fill Ben's spot as a drug dealer. I told them I didn't know what they were talking about. And if they approached me again about any drugs, I was going to report them to Internal Affairs. They walked away in a friendly mood.

I found out a lot that day. I had begun to wonder if it was safe to continue with the drug business. I had gotten used to having extra money in my pocket to do things for my family. I gave my mother money each month to help her out. My brother from down south came up here trying to get a loan to buy furniture for his home. I gave him a small piece of change. And my wife and kids, all they had to do was name it. They got it. No. I can't stop now. I might want to hang in there for another six months. Then maybe find another job. These inmates wouldn't just let me work here and not be in business. They would probably keep the pressure on me forever. But for now, I didn't have the fear of Ben on me anymore.

CHAPTER TEN

Internal Affairs had gotten in contact with the Narcotics Division of the State Police. Sgt. Jerone was assigned to the case. He put two men on the case to work with Henry. After the plan was put together, Henry went back to talk with Ratless. As always, Henry used a private room. "O.K." said Henry. "We got our plan together. Listen closely. We want you to send Wilson to Pimps Town. Here's the address and phone number in case he gets lost. He's going to meet a guy name Mike. Mike will have a pound of marijuana for him and $200. He is to bring the marijuana in and give it to you. You will in turn hand it over to us. No one is to know about this except us and my people. Do you understand all this?"

"Yeah."

"Have him go tomorrow in the evening."

The following day, Ratless gave me my instructions. I'd never heard of Pimps Town. I figures Ratless didn't know because he said the package belonged to someone else. I left work for the day to go figure out my plan.

I called Mike for road directions. When I finished talking with him, I had a clear picture of where to go. I got into my car around 8 p.m. and headed towards Pimps Town. It was only 30 minutes from my home. I was in Pimps Town before I knew it. I turned off the highway onto a road leading to a beach. The road turned into a dead end. I drove up to a telephone booth located on the edge of the boardwalk. I got out of my car. Walked to the booth. Two men were standing there. I identified the red jacket on the one I was told he would be wearing. As I approached the two men, they stopped talking.

"Mike?" I asked.

"Wilson?" He asked.

"Yeah." I answered up.

"I got the stuff in my car. Follow us. By the way, this is my friend Joe."

"Hi Joe." I said in no uncertain manner.

"Hi Wilson." He replied looking me straight into my eyes. Suddenly we started walking toward the car. Mike was driving a late model Buick. He opened the trunk. Inside were all different size packages. He moved a few around until he located mine. He looked it over to make sure it was the right one. Then handed it to me.

"Do you want to buy a couple for yourself?" Mike asked looking directly at me.

"No. Not right now. Maybe some other time."

"If you do, give me a call." He wrote his name and number down on a piece of paper and handed it to me. He said this was a better number to call where he could be reached quicker. He pulled out a large rolls of dollar bills. Two one-hundred-dollar bills were peeled off the top and handed to me. All three of us said good-bye. I walked toward my car looking around as I usually do to see if this was a setup. Not detecting anything suspicious, I got into my car and left for home.

That night when I had bagged up all the weed, I made sixteen one-ounce bags. In the process of weighing them, I skimmed a little from each bag to produce one ounce for a sale to a friend of mine. The next morning, I delivered the package to Ratless. He didn't look the same. Usually he was glad to receive it. This time he took it and put most of it in his pockets and the rest in his briefs.

Curiously. "What's happening?" I asked. "You don't look the same."

"No. I just don't feel well at all. I want to go back to my cell for the rest of the day."

"O.K." I responded. "Take off. Check with the cookhouse officer first." He left. I didn't pay it anymore attention after that.

Two weeks passed. Ratless scheduled another pick up with Mike at the same location in Pimps Town. Between the last trip and this one, I had sold the one ounce to my friend. He liked it so much, I decided on this trip to buy a pound for myself. I figured I could get a real deal from him.

I followed the same instructions. This time, Mike and I was wearing the same identifiable clothing. Joe was also present. He was just tagging along. "I work with a construction crew," said Joe. "We do small jobs around the state. Some of the guys like to smoke every now and then. I was wondering if some time when I'm in your area, I could stop by and pick up a couple ounces from you?"

"Sure. Here's my phone number. When you get ready for it, call me a couple of days in advance. If I don't have it, I'll try to get it for you." Now I directed my attention toward Mike. "Mike, I need to get one of those pounds for myself."

"It's gonna cost you 450."

"Here's 250. Keep the 200 from the package."

"You're on." Mike got two pounds from the trunk. I watched as he went through several packages before handing mine to me. "Thanks." I said.

He made an O.K. motion with the flip of one hand. The both of them got into to Mike's car. I watched as the car rolled away. I took the packages to my car. Both packages were too large for me to push under one seat. I decided to put one under the driver's seat and the other under the passenger's seat. After doing so, I drove off for home.

The next afternoon, I had to work the 12 noon to 8 p.m. shift. I was still in the bed half asleep when Jane and the kids left. I laid there until 9:27 a.m. It was time for me to get up. I had to package Ratless' weed.

TRAPPED BY IMPULSION

Slowly I forced myself out of the bed and into a standing position. Put on my trousers and made my way to the bathroom. I got myself squared away. Next stop, the kitchen. Someone had left part of a half-gallon of orange juice on the table. I fixed some noodle for myself, drank up all the juice and sucked down the noodles.

The weed was as hard as a rock. It must have been chopped off a block. It began to break a part as I pulled on it with my fingers. I started weighing it up into one ounce bags. The telephone rang. On the third ring, I picked it up. "Hello," I said.

"Wilson?" Said a voice on the other end. "Dave told me to call you."

"Dave who?" I asked. "How did you get my phone number?"

"Dave who works in the cookhouse. He got your number when A.B. walked away from his desk. He left the office open and his note book was on his desk with all the telephone numbers in it. He's had your number for a couple of weeks now. Anyway, what I'm calling about, Lieutenant Fink had been talking all morning about busting you with drugs when you come to work today. If you're planning on bringing anything in. I'd let it go until it's safe. I got to go now. Someone's coming. I'm not allowed to use this phone. Later.

The line went dead. I went back to preparing one-ounce bags. So fink made Lieutenant. He was always a real good for nothing type of officer. Now he's shooting off his mouth about what he's planning on doing. I don't know about him. Anyway, if Dave has my phone number, who else and how many others have it? I went on thinking as I worked. I got to play this cool from now on. This weed has got to be delivered. I don't want him on my back. This is my last deal. Things aren't going too well. I finished up all the bagging by 11:20 a.m. The question was now how am I going to get this in? What if fink in really after me? I didn't know he was on to me. This is what I'll do. I'll take the stuff with me but leave it in my car. I'll go in to see if he is for real. If he stops me, I'm clean and I'll bad mouth him so he won't bother me on my second trip in with the weed. If he don't stop me, this is just a test they're putting me through. I put the weed in my car and left for work.

When I pulled up to the prison entrance, I stopped. If it's true about the bust, they can search my car if it's on government property. I decided to park on a back street out of sight of the tower guards. I found a parking space one block away. I walked to the prison entrance, staying close to the building. I entered the prison. Everyone was busy doing their normal routine. I made my way to the check point. The guard patted me down and passed me through. I went straight to my work area. Ratless was working. He stopped when he saw me. He walked toward my direction.

"I didn't know how to get in contact with you." He said. "Lt. Fink has been shooting off his mouth. If you brought in the weed, good. If you didn't, we can wait."

"I got the stuff in my car. Someone called my house a little while age to tip me off. The sooner I get it to you the better off I'll feel. This is my last trip. I feel things are closing in on me."

"Things will get better. Take off for a couple of weeks. Don't shut me down. We're making money. There's still things I want to do for my family with the money."

"You got to find another person to help you with your means. If I get busted, I'm subject to lose my job and possibly get some time in jail."

"You won't go to jail."

"How can you be so sure? You're an inmate. You can't protect me from the officers or the administration. If you tell me you can save me, that's just like you telling me you're going to send ice to hell because they need ice water."

There was silence.

I left the bakery to go up to the officer's dining room. When I arrived I noticed Lt. Fink was eating. He looked in my direction but said nothing to me. I wanted to say something to him but the time wasn't right. I grabbed a sandwich, and sat near a corner in plain view of him.

When I was half-way through my sandwich, he got up with two of his officer friends and left. At that point I realized he was all mouth all the time. I finished my sandwich, then went to my car to get Ratless' weed. I has no problem getting out of the building.

2 p.m.

The second shift officers were starting to come on. I passed a few of them on my way to my car. I unlocked the door and got inside. As I sat, I could see officers walking toward me. I decided to drive about four or five blocks away so I wouldn't be seen. I drive to a small parking lot next to a Deli. I took off my shoes and began to load up. The owner of the car I had parked next to came out of the Deli to get into his car. I stopped handling the weed. He looked at me. I looked back. I rolled down my window to get some air. He loaded packages into the trunk of his car and walked around to the driver's side. Got in. Took another look at me. Started up his car and drove off. I wondered if I looked suspicious. Who cares? I'll have this stuff all packed in a few minutes and I'll be gone. I managed to get my shoes filled. I couldn't move my legs the way I wanted to. I got my foot partly in the shoe. Now I couldn't tie them up. My legs kept banging against the dash board. The steering wheel was holding my chest back so I couldn't lean forward. I began to struggle with the shoes. This wasn't getting it. I opened the car door. I placed one shoe on the ground. I did the same with the other shoe. Now that I had them both on, I stood up to pack them inside. Oh no. A stick was sticking up in the center of my left foot. I had to sit down to take off my shoe to readjust the package. I got up again. Better this time. I sat down to tie up my laces. I had four one-ounce packs left. I tried to get them in my briefs but they wouldn't go in while I was in the sitting position. With my trousers half-fastened, I started walking until I was sure no one was watching me. I pushed the packs, one at a time into my briefs. I was set to go. I walked back to my car, got in and drove back to my same parking space. The lobby was filled with officers. LT. Fink was there.

He had his back to me. I made my way through the crowd and over to the entrance. The officer didn't pat me down. He let me go straight through. Ratless was not in the cookhouse. I had to hold onto the stuff for one hour and twenty five minutes until he came down for dinner. I continued to make myself visible. No one had missed me.

4:15 p.m.

Chow started. Ratless' block was the first group to come down. By now, I had taken all the weed out of my shoes and had it around my waist in order to make a quick transfer. I spotted him coming in. He came to the gate leading to the kitchen. He called the officer in the kitchen to come to the gate. When the officer arrived, Ratless told him he needed to get his spoon and cup. The officer was giving him a hard time. I walked over to them.

"It's O.K. officer," I said. "I'll stay with him until he gets his stuff. I won't let him out of my sight. I'll bring him back to you to let out."

"O.K.," said the officer. "Make it quick. He's not supposed to be down here."

"O.K."

Ratless came in. We walked straight to the bakery. This seemed to be the only safe place in the kitchen. All other areas either had cooks, officers or inmates in them. I locked the gate once we were inside. "Move those bread racks so no one will see us." I said. "I have the whole thing around my waist. So be as quick as you can with this transfer."

"I will." He had problems moving the racks. Some of the wheels were missing. I had to give him a hand. We made the transfer in about two minutes. I gave him a spoon and cup that had been in the bakery.

"I appreciate this," said Ratless. "I won't have any problems passing these off. All the guys are out."

"Remember what I said. This is your last trip."

"O.K."

We both left the bakery. I took him to the officer at the kitchen gate. He let him out.

CHAPTER ELEVEN

Henry had left for home earlier this day. He had heard about Lt. Fink. This had made him very angry. He figured I had gotten word and left the stuff home. In fact, he had called LT. Fink to his office to ball him out for passing rumors. Lt. Fink promised to keep his mouth closed from now on.

6 p.m.

It was time to go to the yard. Henry had not picked up the weed from Ratless. He decided since he was an inmate already in prison, what could Henry do to him if he sold the weed. I'm going to make them pay since I can't get out was Ratless' plan.

Ratless took the whole pound to the yard. He had no problem getting it pass the officer and into the yard. He set up a spot. "Best herb in the joint." He said. "Anybody who's down with it. I'm going to make you a deal. Instead of charging you $125 for one ounce, as a quick sale. I'm giving $25 off. Yes, for only $100 you can have the best weed known to mankind. Form a line on my right. You don't have to pay now. Have someone on the street send a check to my people. That's all you need to do."

They lined up. Some of the inmates went in together on one ounce. Ratless refused to sell to three inmates because they had already owed him and were months behind in paying up. The whole pound was passed off.

The next morning when Henry came to work, he stopped by his informer's mailbox to see if any notes were left for him. There were several. All pertaining to Ratless' big sale in the yard last night. He immediately went to Ratless' cell. He didn't care who saw him. "Ratless. You got my stuff?"

"No. Somebody beat me for it when I went to supper yesterday."

"That ain't what I heard."

"What did they tell you?"

"I heard you had a sale in the yard. You sold the whole pound by the ounce. Pack up. I'm sending you to solitary confinement."

"You ain't got nothing on me. That's only hearsay."

"I'm going to shake the whole prison down to retrieve that weed."

"That's on you."

Henry knew he was right. This was a secret deal. He could get the prison system in trouble for what had gone down with the weed. Henry went to the chief's office. He told him he had gotten word that three pounds of weed had gotten loose in the prison. He requested a full shake down and full search be conducted. The prison was shut down for twenty-four hours. No weed was recovered. This was Henry's lost.

Ratless was taken to solitary confinement for two days. Afterwards, he was transferred to another prison. Henry had kept his word. No charges were brought against Ratless. After all, he had put Wilson in their hands. Before Ratless left, he wrote me a letter. It was delivered by one of his friends.

The letter read:

> *Wilson. It ain't every day that I thank someone for helping me. I must confess I let you down. Sometime ago I set you up for more*

money and to save myself. It is best that you stop bringing in weed immediately. Henry knows about you and the operation. I told him somethings. The informers told him the rest. I'm surprised they haven't nailed you by now. Maybe they're playing games with you. I didn't sign anything and I won't. You can count on me to keep my mouth shut from here on. I will deny anything they say I said about you or did with you. Later.

This is why he was acting strange. And Henry kept his eyes on me. It was all coming together now. Lt. Fink was really trying to warn me. I thought he was being a loud mouth. Yeah. They all probably know the whole deal. I worked the whole day without any interruptions. However, I did think a lot about my situation.

That evening as I drove home, I turned onto Shadow Road. About an eighth of a mile down the road, I could see a road check. I pulled over to the side of the road and stopped. This road has never had a road check in the past ten years since I have been traveling on this road. First I thought they might be checking to see what time I usually travel this way, or to see if my address matches between my job and my driver's license. Then it occurred to me that a drunk driving check might be underway. I decided to drive through to see what was going on. As I approached the standing officers on the roadway, a line of orange colored cones forced me onto the right lane. There was a police car sitting off the road behind a clump of bushes to prevent anyone from turning around. I stopped next to the officer.

"Good evening," said the first officer.

"Good evening," I responded.

He shined his flash light into my car while he looked around. "O.K., drive up to the next officer." I followed instructions. About fifty feet up ahead stood the second officer. I drove up to him and stopped.

"Can I see your driver's license?"

"Do you want my insurance card and registration?"

"No, just your license."

At that point, I took out my license, handed it to him.

He handed some papers to me saying. "Here is some material on drunk driving."

I took it and placed it on the passenger's seat. The second officer walked over to a third officer. He showed him my license. Just ahead was a bank parking lot where several officers were talking with other drivers. A lady with three children got out of her car. An officer led the three to a police car near the road. They entered and the driver drove it away.

The second officer walked back to my car. "Drive over to the parking lot," he said while looking around the inside of my car.

As I drove over, he followed me on foot. I watched as he went over to a police car where two officers were operating a small machine. I begin to wonder what is causing the problem. Why were they taking so long to let me drive throw. After all, they didn't search my car. Didn't put me through any test. I had not been drinking or on drugs. I didn't have any open containers in my car. I definitely didn't have any drugs in my car. I looked around. There was six other vehicles parked nearby that they found drugs inside. About three minutes later, the officer came to my car.

"Here you are Mr. Wilson." He said while handing my license back to me.

"Are there any problems?"

"No. You're okay to go. Thanks for being patient."

I drove off for home.

When I arrived, I told Jane about what had happened.

"They have been out there since 5:15 this evening."

"Wednesday sure is an odd day to hold this. Most people drink on the weekends when they don't have to work and have money to burn."

The next afternoon when I arrived at home, Jane was in the kitchen cooking. "A guy name Joe called," she said. "He left this number. It's on top of the microwave oven. He said call him as soon as you get home."

I picked up the piece of paper. Looked the number over closely. Then put it back on top of the microwave. "Did he say anything else?"

"No. Just call him."

About two hours later, the phone rang. Jane answered it. I was busy fixing Bill's bike. She came out into the garage. "Joe's on the phone. What should I tell him?"

"Tell him to hold on. I'll be right there."

I tightened the last screw. Then went to answer the phone. "Joe?"

"Yeah, this is joe. Do you remember us talking about you selling me some weed?"

"Yeah. I remember."

"If it's all possible. I would like to get two ounces tomorrow evening. Would that be okay with you?"

"Sure. I'll have it. What time will you be coming around?"

"How about 7:30 p.m."

"How about making it around 8?"

"That's okay, too."

"I'll see you then."

Jane had gone upstairs to roll up her hair. I went upstairs to get a glass of orange juice. I drank a full glass straight down. It was good and cold. I turned out the light. Then went into the bedroom.

"Who's Joe?"

"Oh. He's a friend of mine."

"One of your on-the-road friends?"

"I guess you could say that."

"Don't you think they might be setting you up for whatever you're doing? I worry about you."

"It's okay. These guys are about the same thing."

We didn't talk about it anymore. I crawled into bed. I watched television until I fell asleep.

The next evening when I drove from work going home, the drunk driving check was not set up. I arrived at my home to find Joe's car outside. I pulled onto the driveway. Got out of my car. I watched as Joe got out of his car. He walked over to me.

"Good timing." He said. "I've been waiting about five minutes. I didn't see your car when I pulled up. Plus it wasn't quite eight yet. So I decided to sit here for a few minutes."

"You probably did the best thing. If you had knocked on my door, you would have found that I wasn't home anyway. My wife would have told you to wait outside. She never lets people in she doesn't know.

"My wife would have done the same thing too." "Let's go inside. We walked up the steps to the landing. "Wait here a minute while I see if she is dressed." I went into the house leaving the door open. Down at the end of the short hallway our bedroom door was open. I walked in. Jane was sitting on the edge of the bed putting curlers in her hair. "I brought someone into our home."

"Close the door." She said quickly.

"I will. I was just checking to see if you had any clothing on." I closed the door. Walked back to the front door to tell Joe to come in. He followed me into the kitchen. I got out the two ounces from a cabinet over the refrigerator. It was in a brown bag. I handed it to him. He took it out of the bag. Looked it over closely. Bounced it in his hand a couple of times and then placed it back into the bag.

"Looks and feels okay to me. How much do you want for it?"

"Give me 150."

He reached into his pocket. Took out a large roll of dollar bills. Peeled off three fifties and handed over to me.

"Thanks." I said.

"If this is anything like what Mike had, the guys are sure to like it. You sure have a nice home."

"Thanks."

"Do you have any kids?"

"Yeah. Two boys. Ages, five and nine."

"Look. I have to be going. If this works out okay, I'll get in touch with you later about getting more."

I walked him to the door. Watched as he walked to his car in the poorly lighted night. He got inside and drove away. I went back into the house. Jane came out to fix my dinner. She talked on the phone as we ate. Afterwards, went into our bed room to watch television until I fell asleep. She stayed in the kitchen.

By now, I had sold nine of the sixteen ounces. I wouldn't have any problems selling the rest. My friend had told me it was good. I had no other way of knowing. After all, I nor Jane smoked the stuff. I was in it for the bucks. After I sell the rest,, I had planned to quit. I would have to find another way to continue to make money. Besides, the word was out on me. I couldn't deal in the prison anymore. In fact, I might be getting busted any day now according to what Ratless had written to me. Yeah, I'm going to cool it.

CHAPTER TWELVE

During the next couple of weeks, I continued to work at the prison. I had fired Dick and Buck. They had gotten lazy and started going crazy and stopped coming to work every day. I was faced with a new crew. Training was coming along slowly. This crew wasn't as interested in baking as the first crew. I decided to quit working as a baker to become a cook.

I had known all the cooks from day one. I just never had the time to hang around them. They didn't come out to tell me directly, but I had known all along through inmates talking. Some of the cooks were into the same thing I was into.

John was the chief cook. Blake was just a cook. Both of them were known for bringing in small amounts of any type of drugs. Now that I was working with them, I had more of an opportunity to communicate with them. Both of them must have known about me. John came up to me one day.

"Did you know my house was raided about two weeks ago?" Said John.

"No. I didn't know anything about that."

"Yeah. They raided Blake's house last week too. Both times it was the State Police. They came at four in the morning and kicked our door in. I don't keep anything in my house anyway. If you got anything, you better get rid of it."

"Yeah. I'll do that."

While we continued to talk, there was a disturbance going on in the supply storage room. Blake had gotten into a fight with one of the inmates. I could hear the inmate talking loud to Blake."

"I want my money, and I want it within 24 hours or you belong to me."

"I ain't giving you a damn thing. You got what you paid for."

Two officers rushed passed us going toward that area. They had night sticks and hand cuffs in their hands. A couple of minutes later, they came back holding Blake by the arm. His eyes were all glassy and he had trouble walking straight.

Everyone knew Blake was a drug addict. At times he would cheat inmates out of their drugs and money. For two or three days after pay day, he would be so high he wouldn't call in or come to work. I don't know how he kept his job. Several times inmates would ask me to talk with him about his problem. I told them I was neutral. I wouldn't have anything to do with it. On the other hand, john was cool. He did drugs when he wasn't working. He never got in any scraps with the people he dealt with.

Two hours later, word had gotten back to us that Blake had been suspended. They found drugs on his person. Before they could get them away from him. He swallowed them. This left John and myself to work the inmates. We worked together. We had gotten the job done by 7:30 p.m. that evening.

Instead of going straight home that evening, John and I decided we would go to the local bar for a few drinks. We walked outside and down to the corner bar. The place was blasting with music as we walked in. Most of the tables were filled. We decided to sit at the bar. The bar tender came over to us.

"What'll you have?" He asked.

"I'll have a glass of your coldest beer." I said.

"I'll have the same." Said John. As I looked around, I saw a few people were dancing to the music. The television was on, but the sound was turned down low.

"I think Blake went too far this time." Said John.

"Yeah. He has to learn how to control his habit."

"He ain't gonna learn anything. Those drugs got him going. If he don't get fired, those inmates are gonna kill him." The bartender returned with our beers. I placed a ten-dollar bill on the counter. The bartender took it. We took a sip and began to munch on the popcorn and peanuts sitting on the bar in front of us. The bartender returned. He laid my change on the counter in front of me.

"What Ben did was bad news," I said.

"You know, he would have only gotten one year in solitary confinement and probably lost all his good time."

"I guess he hung up because in solitary confinement, all you do is just sit around day after day, night after night."

"No. They got it better than that. He can have his television and radio. He gets yard twice a week. And he can work cleaning up or in the kitchen after sixty days."

"This job don't pay enough for the mess we have to put up with."

John moved closer to me so I could hear him better. "I got a job offer from the army base. I've been thinking about taking it. It's a slight pay cut but it's less of a hassle."

"Good for you, John," I said. "I haven't started looking yet. But I think I need a change of scenery."

"By the way. What's up with Lt. Fink?"

"I don't know. He's either trying to blow my game or he's trying to tip me off. Well, I only came for one drink. I have to be going. There's things I have to be doing before I go to bed."

"Yeah. Me too. I have to meet someone at 10:30 this evening."

We drank up. I picked up my change all except for one dollar. We walked outside. "I'll see you tomorrow at work." I said.

"O.K. Take care."

I got into my car and drive my way out of the parking lot. John was still sitting in his car when I left.

I parked my car in my driveway. It had gotten darker by now. The light on the landing was on. I had no problem finding the right keys for the door. I entered the house. As I closed the door behind me, Jane began talking to me.

"There was a note in the mailbox. Some guy named Joe left it. He wants you to call him as soon as you get home."

"I'll call him later." I went into my bedroom to change clothes.

"Do you want something to eat?"

"Yeah. Whatever you fix will be okay with me." About four minutes later, I returned to the kitchen. I began to eat. The phone rang. I picked it up. "Hello?" I said.

"Wilson. Is this Joe?"

"Yeah. What's up?"

"Just chillin."

"My friends asked me to stop by tomorrow for a quarter pound."

"Yeah. Come by early."

"O.K. See you then."

I hung up. "That was Joe." After eating dinner, I went down stairs to say hello to my kids. Then came back up to take a shower and I got ready for bed.

"That's the whole story." I said.

The two officers who were searching my bedroom came into the dining room. Both were carrying stuff which they placed on the table. There were numerous items; a stack of account records; a signed check from a inmate; a small box of phone numbers and three address books; $245 in cash; a cigar box filled with pipes, papers, nickel bags and plastic cigar tubes filled with marijuana.

"Is there anymore?" Asked Sgt. Jerone.

Joe had seen me get the quarter-pound from over the refrigerator. He must have told Sgt. Jerone because he went straight to the spot. Pulled out the bag with four ounces. He brought it to the dining room table. Laid it with the other items. An officer came from downstairs carrying my weighing scale and another quarter-pound. There were other items found during the search, but Sgt. Jerone told them to put them back because those were not the type of things they were after. Sgt. Jerone looked at some of the phone numbers and names. "Are these some of the people who supply you with the marijuana?"

"Yeah."

"Where do they live?"

"All over the state."

"How do you get in contact with them?"

"I only call them when an inmate has already talked with them. He tells them to expect a call from me. Then I call. If I was to call them now, they probably wouldn't give me anything. I have to call them at certain times."

"Do you go to their house?"

"No. I meet them at gas stations, beaches, stores and other designated spots. The two houses I told you I went to, those people didn't live there."

"Do you think you can find those houses again?"

"Yeah. But they don't live there any longer. The last time I met with them, it was at a different location. It's getting late. What time will I be allowed to leave for work?"

"You won't be going to work today. I think they already know that. Put on the rest of your clothes?"

The house was completely silent. I rose up from the table and went into my bedroom. An officer followed me. I got fully dressed. He followed me back into the dining room. Sgt. Jerone told the officers to continue to search for whatever they could find. Then come to the township police station. "We're going to the police station," he told me. "One of you officers look outside to see if any of the neighbors are watching the house. We don't want to draw any more attention than necessary." The officer went out to look around. "I'm going to have to put these handcuffs on you."

"Do you have to? I'm not going to run away."

"I have to. This is normal procedure."

I held out my hands. He snapped the cuffs around my wrist.

The officer went outside, looked around and returned. "It's okay," he said.

Sgt. Jerone led me down the flight of steps. We stopped at the door. Two officers followed close behind us. Sgt. Jerone stepped outside onto the landing. He looked around. Then signaled for us to come outside. He started walking toward one of the last cars. I followed. Three officers walked behind me. Sgt. Jerone opened the back door. I got in. One officer got in to sit on my left and one on my right. Sgt. Jerone and the officer got into the front seat. He backed out of the driveway. Off we went toward the police station.

Jane had dropped the kids off at school. Then she went straight to her job. At work, she became very dissatisfied with the way things had gone down at the house. She remembered a couple of years back, her girlfriend's husband had gotten busted with fifty pounds of weed. He had this lawyer who got him off with a fine. She decided this was the best move to make. She called her and was given all the necessary information. When she called the lawyer, he was not in his office. She left her name and number where she could be reached. Two hours later, the lawyer called.

"Mrs. Wilson. You called my office?"

"Yes I did. My husband got locked up this morning for possessing a controlled dangerous substance. I need a lawyer for him. You were recommended by my girlfriend whose husband you defended for having fifty pounds of marijuana."

"Yes. I remember him. If you can give me $2,500 today, I'll get started on his case right away."

"Give me one hour to have it in your office."

"I'll see you then. Good bye."

"Good bye." After hanging up, she went straight to her boss' office, told him she had some important business that had to be taken care of immediately and needed the rest of the day off. He gave her the okay. She immediately left.

When she arrived at home, it was locked and all the officers were gone. She entered the house to find everything in its place. The officers put back all the stuff they had taken out of the closets and draws. She looked in the bedroom night-stand draw for the bankbook. All four of them were gone. They must have taken them during the shake-down. She called the lawyer's office to tell him what had happened. Then she decided to sit back to wait for me to call.

CHAPTER THIRTEEN

The three-minute ride to the township police station was in total silence. I was handcuffed during the entire trip. The unmarked car parked in a space not far from a door leading to a side entrance. We got out of the car and entered with Sgt. Jerone leading the way. I was walking right behind him. The hallway was long. There were several people moving about. We walked almost halfway down it before going through a side door leading to a set of stairs. At the bottom of the steps was another long hallway. We went into Sgt. Jerone's office. There were three other plain-clothes officers at work. Sgt. Jerone went to sit behind his desk. I was told to take a seat next to it. One of the officers in the group removed my handcuffs.

"We going to take your fingerprints and picture." Said Sgt. Jerone. He looked at some papers on his desk. Then handed a few of them to the officer who removed my handcuffs. "Take him to the fingerprinting room," he said to the officer with the papers.

We walked pass two officers before making a right turn and down another short hallway. On the corner was the fingerprinting room. I was stopped at the doorway even though the door was open. Next to it were five cells about five feet across and six feet deep. The area had poor lighting. All the cells were empty. An officer in uniform walked past going into the room. He set up the equipment then motioned for me to enter. I walked to the fingerprinting equipment. He made prints of my fingers from both hands. Afterwards, he directed me to a sink where he poured some sort of liquid over my hands. Then told me to clean them. Next we moved to a camera area. I sat on a stool facing the camera. He gave me this board with my name and lots of numbers on it to hold up to my chest. After taking several pictures, he took the board.

Sgt. Jerone stepped into the room. He asked me to follow him. We went upstairs to a small room. We went in. He closed the door behind us. Again he sat behind a desk. I sat directly in front of it this time.

He started questioning me. "What happened to the money you made from the trips?"

"I didn't collect it all. They still owe me most of it. I should be receiving most of the checks soon."

The door opened. Henry and another investigator from the prison walked in with two uniform officers. Sgt. Jerone got up from behind the desk to go sit in a chair next to the wall. Henry now took the seat behind the desk. His assistant stood holding a stack of files.

"You messed up our whole system," said Henry. "We got enough on you to lock you up for 135 years. Do you want to tell us all about it? Or do we have to press for the whole 135 years."

"If you're talking about giving me 135 years, why should I talk? I won't live to the end of my sentence. I don't really care at this point what you do."

"Both of you take it easy," said Sgt. Jerone. "Henry, he's willing to cooperate, but if that's the best approach you can make, don't expect anything out of him."

"All right." Henry said. His assistant took out a stack of papers that he had taken from my house. He placed the top sheet in front of me that contained initials and numbers. "Whose initials are these? And what do these numbers mean?"

"The numbers under the initials are what is owed to me by the owners of the initials."

"Whom do they belong to?"

"The B.S. belongs to Ben. The R.T. belongs to Ratless. The M.E. is mine. I owe money to someone. The other letters are there to throw off anyone who sees this paper if it falls into the wrong hands."

"You're lying."

"If you think I'm lying, you tell me about this paper?"

The other officer placed a check on the desk in front of me.

"Is this your hand writing on the back of this check?"

Henry pushed the check up close to my front.

"No. Ben signed all the checks sent to me by the inmates."

"That don't look like his hand writing."

"I gave the checks to him. He took them away and brought them back signed. I assumed he did all the signing."

"What about Ratless? How much did he pay you for giving him drugs?"

"About $100 per trip."

"Did you know he was making almost $3,000 a month dealing drugs? And all you was getting was only a $100? You're a real sucker."

"I don't have to take this off you."

"They should give you 135 years. If you give us all the names of the guys you're supplying drugs, we'll try to have your sentence reduced to 12 years. Do you recognize any of these faces?"

Henry placed photo after photo in front of me. I failed to recognize any of them. It had been a long day for me. It was now approaching 1 p.m. "I'm tired of answering questions. I'm not talking anymore today."

"You can't quit on us."

"Bull. Who says I can't. You can't make me talk. You should have come to my home this morning with the officers."

"I think he's right," said Sgt. Jerone.

O.K., said Henry. "Here's a letter from the Warden."

I took the letter and read it over. It said I was temporarily suspended from my job pending the outcome of a hearing. I would be notified when to appear, time and place. Henry and his assistant placed all the papers back into their file envelopes. They tied them together. Henry went to open the door and returned to help his assistant pick up the files. They left. Sgt. Jerone placed the handcuffs back onto my wrist. He and I left the building and I was seated into his back seat of his car.

"Where we going?" I asked.

"I'm taking you back downtown." He started the car and drove out of the parking lot. "You're in a lot of trouble whether you realize it or not. I'm going to request that the judge set you're bail at $50,000."

I didn't know if that was good of bad. "I don't understand why everyone is so down on me. Maybe what I did was wrong, but it wasn't that bad. It isn't like I was giving weed to kids or that I killed someone. These were criminal adults. Everyone agreed to the transactions. Almost everyone smokes weed. They were smoking weed in prisons long before I got there. I'm gone from there now. And they'll still be smoking up a storm and the prison officials know it."

"What you did was wrong. You broke the law. It's a crime. You have to answer for what you did. You can't supply inmates with drugs and making money from what you were doing at the same time. I got to do my job."

"Yeah. I realize you have to do your job. I'm not holding anything against you."

"No more questions."

We rode the rest of the way in silence. Finally, we reached the downtown police station. He pulled up to a screened in metal door. It seemed to automatically go up. The car moved inside and the door came down just as it went up. Sgt. Jerone pulled into a parking space. He got out of the car and came around to my side and removed my handcuffs. I climbed out of the car and we walked up a few steps to a small office overlooking the parking area. When we entered, he told the officer I was staying. I was placed in a holding cell by another officer. I was the only one in there. He continued talking to the officer and after a few minutes Sgt. Jerone came over to where I was.

"The judge is still here," he said. "I'm going to get him to post bail on you." An officer let me out. Sgt. Jerone placed the cuffs back onto my wrist. We walked down a long hallway leading to the court house. It was a direct underground route from one building to another. We came out on the other end where a lot of people were walking around. He led me into a small courtroom where the judge was already seated on the bench. Sgt. Jerone said something to the prosecutor. The prosecutor approached the bench. He red my charges to the judge. Then he requested the judge post a $50,000 cash bail. He did so. I was taken back to where he put the cuffs on me.

"I have $245 of yours that we picked up in your house."

"It's part of my check. Can you give it to my wife so she can buy food?"

"No. I'll put it in your account here."

"Don't do that. It'll take her days to get that money back if it's put into an account."

"Here's what I'll do. I'll tell them not to lock it up if you are sure she'll come pick it up."

"She will. I'll call her first chance I get."

If that's the best you can do, I'll go along with it. You'll have to spend the weekend here. I'll be back tomorrow."

He left. This meant I would be here Friday night, Saturday, Sunday and most of Monday. I sat for about a half hour thinking about the events that had taken place so far today. My cousin glanced in my direction as he walked pass. He immediately took a back step to return. He looked at me in complete surprise.

"Jack. Is that you?"

"Yeah." I said while looking between sad and mad.

"What the heck happened to you?"

"It's a long story. I didn't know you were working here."

"Yeah. I've been working here for about 3 years. It's great seeing you. But not in here." He hunched his shoulders and walked away.

By now the time was approaching 3:30. I hadn't eaten or drank anything except for the glass of orange juice Sgt. Jerone poured for me this morning. No one thought to offer me anything to eat or drink. I don't think they cared.

A correction officer came to my cell. He opened it and told me to come with him. We walked to an area that looked like a clothing storage room. The officer I was with turned me over to the Sgt. behind the counter.

"Take off everything and lay them on the counter," he said.

I did as he instructed.

"The shower is over there. Here's soap and a towel. Use this cream on your hair."

I started toward the shower.

"When you finish, put on these clothes and slippers. And when you get them on, sign this slip saying these articles belong to you."

He pointed in the direction of the slip. "The $245 will be kept separate. Sign this slip now."

I looked over the slip. "This slip says $255. I only have $245 in all."

He recounted the money. Then made out a new slip. "Thanks. You saved me $10. He called another officer to take me to the cell area after I had showered. I was given a tooth brush, tooth paste, face cloth and a bar of soap.

We rode the elevator to the fourth floor. We went through a double set of electronic doors. Now we were in a medium-size cell block area. To my left was a glass-enclosed booth with two officers inside. The officer with me gave one of them some papers. An officer came out of the booth with two sheets, a blanket, a pillow and pillow case. He handed them to me. I looked around. The area consisted of two levels of cells. All about 4 1/2 feet by 6 1/2 feet inside. All the cells ran along three sides of the cell block.

"You have cell number 12 on the second floor."

I looked toward the second floor just to see number 12's bars slide back to open. I walked through the seating area, passing inmates watching television and playing cards sitting around metal dining tables. I entered the cell to make myself at home for the next few days. The first thing I did was make up my bed. It was a metal slab with a four inch thick mattress. I laid on it to see how it felt. It was softer than it looked.

An announcement came over the intercom saying dinner was ready to be served. Immediately I started hearing the sound of steel doors sliding open, one at a time. My door was already open. I went down to get in the chow line. I moved along with the rest of the inmates until I reached the serving area. A metal plate was handed to me as I moved along in line with my plate in front of me. Food handlers placed large servings of food on it. The food didn't look too inviting but I accepted it. I moved off the end of the line to take a vacant seat near the television. There were three guys sitting at the table who didn't say a word. Steam was coming from my stew beef. I began to stir it with my spoon. A dead fly surfaced as I moved the stew around. At first I didn't believe it, but then I could see the wings. I pushed the plate away.

"What the matter?" asked one of the guys.

"There's flies in my stew."

"Take them out. There's always something in it. We get some type of stew or sauce all the time. Look at it this way. That's more meat in it. I think they give us this to hide whatever falls in the food."

"Well, I don't want it and I don't have to eat it."

"If you stay here long enough, you'll either eat it or starve. Can I have yours?"

"Take it. I'll just have to starve." I got up and went to the telephone hanging on the wall to call Jane. The operating instructions stated, *all calls are to be made person-to-person. Dial the operator for assistance.* I did. The phone rang. Bill answered. In the background it sounded like the house was filled with people. Plus the television was on.

"Hello," Bill answered.

"Hi, Bill. Where's mommy? Let me speak with her."

"Where you at?" He asked.

"I'll have to tell you later. First let me speak with your mother."

"Mom, Dad want to talk with you." I could hear him shouting.

She took the phone. "Jack, I tried to get you a lawyer but I couldn't get any money out of the bank. Our bank books are gone."

"Go to the bank first thing in the morning and report the books as missing. See if they will let you withdraw any money you need. If you need forms signed by me, give them to Smith on Spring Street. He works here."

"O.K. But instead of giving them to him, I'll find out when visiting hours are. I'll bring them myself."

"Just remember if you have any problems, be sure to give them to him. I hear a lot of voices. You got company?"

"Yeah. My parents and a few of my girlfriends."

"Oh. Before I forget, check with the desk. They have $245 for you. I have to go for now. I'll call every evening around 7 to 7:30. Tell your people I said, 'hello'. And tell Bill and Sam I'll be home on Monday or Tuesday."

"They'll really be glad to see you and so will I."

"Me too. I'll see you soon." I hung up and went back to the table where I lift my food. I sat down to watch television.

"What you here for," asked one of the guys.

"Handling drugs. I got a $50,000 Cash bail."

"Handling Drugs? You aint got no charge, man. Most of the guys are in here for drug dealing. That $50,000 bail will be reduced to $10,000 with 10% on Monday. My bail is $75. I ain't got no money. That's why I'm still here."

"I hope to be out of here by Monday or Tuesday at the latest."

He when back to talking with his friends. I sat until 11 p.m. watching television and listening to guys talking about their crimes, people who got out and returned and who's fooling around with whose girlfriend.

At eleven, the television was turned off. We were all told to go into our cell for the night. I went up the steps to my cell. As I entered my cell, I could hear cell doors opening and closing. I walked to my bed and sat on it. The cell block area was quiet except for the clinging of cell doors. I started developing claustrophobia as the cling got closer. I watched my cell door close. I sat feeling like a caged animal. It seemed like all the ventilation was cut off. I started feeling hot. I felt my blood pressure rising. I called for the officer but no one came. I walked back and forth in my cell trying to think of a way to get some fresh air. I was getting hotter. I walked over to the window, which was one foot wide to five feet high. I could see a few cars passing and several large, empty parking lots. I placed my face against the glass. The cold glass seemed to cool off part of my face. Immediately I started coming back to my senses. Then I walked over to my sink. Turned on the cold water. When I thought it was at its coldest point, I started putting it on my face and head. I kept it up until I felt normal again. I turns off the water and dried off with my face cloth. I laid on my bed. I could hear guys talking and calling each other's name. I had a busy day. Now I was drifting off to sleep.

Off and on during the night, I would wake up. I could still hear guys talking and laughing. I didn't know how they could enjoy themselves when they had charges facing them. On the other hand. If you were a repeated offender, going in and out of jail was a way of life. And to some, being in jail was almost equal to being out on the streets.

CHAPTER FOURTEEN

The lights came on. I could hear the sound of moving cell doors. This woke me up. My cell door opened but I didn't move from my spot in bed. I went back to sleep. I was awakened a short time later by some guy standing in front of my cell calling to me. "Hey man. You eating this morning?"

"No. I don't do breakfast in the morning," I said without opening my eyes.

"Can I have yours?"

"Yeah. You can have mine every morning. Now go away." He left. I rolled over and went back to sleep.

It must have been around 10 a.m. when I was awakened again. This time it was an officer. "Wilson. Put your clothes on. You got to get fingerprinted and your picture taken." I got up, put on my clothes. I brushed my teeth and washed my face. He watched the whole time. After I finished up, we walked down the steps and over to the glass booth. The officer tapped on the glass. He signaled for the officer inside to open the sliding door to let us out. I followed him to an elevator. We stepped on and rode down to the bottom exist. He led me to a small room. It took the officer inside about ten minutes to take my fingerprints and picture. I was taken back toward my cell block. Instead of going into my cell, I decided to sit with the guys and watch television.

"I see you made the front page," said an inmate sitting near me reading today's newspaper. "You the cook aren't you?"

"Yeah. What did it say?"

"Here. Read it for yourself."

I read the article. It tried to build me up as a major drug dealer at the prison. It described me as having in my possession two pounds of marijuana when really I only had less than a pound. I was being held on $50,000 cash bail in the County Detention Center. I read the rest of the paper and passed it on. They were really trying to blow this up.

By now, it was lunchtime. The steel sliding door opened. Five inmates wearing white clothing came in pushing two large carts of hot food. They rolled the carts over to the serving area and began setting up the line. I sat and watched until they had it set up. The officer called us over. Once again I decided to give the food another try. I went through the line. This time spaghetti was served along with canned fruit, some type of greens and a salad. I took a seat in the same spot where I had my last meal. I picked through my spaghetti for what I could find. I didn't trust the cooks after last night's meal. Right on time. Here it was. A long black hair in my spaghetti. That's it, I said to myself. They don't have to worry about me when it comes to their food rations. This convinced me that I had two choices. Let them kill me or I could starve and kill myself. I was now determined to starve it out. I pushed my food to the center of the table. The other guys at the table split it up. I sat and continued to watch television. My name was called over the intercom to report to the glass booth. There was a lady from the Public Defender's office who was interested in my financial status. I went with her into a small room. An officer followed us inside and closed the door behind us while I took a seat with her facing us.

"I'm here to help you. Are you presently working?"

"No. Can't you see I'm in jail?" I thought that was a dumb question. I wondered how many more of these type of questions do she intent to throw at me.

"Do you have a lawyer?"

"Yes. If I didn't. I certainly wouldn't use a Public Defender. As far as I'm concerned, they're in training. They don't present themselves well and they lose more cases then they win."

She made no comment. Then suddenly she said, "I want a list of all your assets. This means property, money in the bank and stocks if you have any. I have to inform you if you give me any false statements, you could be prosecuted. These papers are considered legal documents."

"I don't know the value of by home. I couldn't even guess. I have two cars. One with scratches and the other with dents. Your guess is as good as mine as to the values. As for money in the bank, check with the State Police. They took the books. I don't know if the money now belongs to me or to them."

"You're not being very cooperative."

"Hey. I did the best I could do. You guys are in the driver's seat now. The law enforcement agency has the keys to my home, cars, and my bank books. If you're going to get me out today, I'll try a little harder. If not. Good Day miss."

"I'll be back this evening for sure to let you know if it's possible for you to get out soon." She waved to the officer. He came. I went back to my cell. She had another inmate called in.

Sgt. Jerone had come to visit me while I was being interviewed. He was waiting in the glass enclosure. He waved to me as I entered the cell block. I waited for him to come out to me. He called me back to the other side of the door. The door closed behind me.

"How's things been going?" He asked.

"O.K. But they could be better."

"I have some pictures I want you to see."

He took out three pictures. Handed them to me. The men looked almost a like.

"Do you remember having any dealings with this guy or any of these guys?"

"Yes. They look like Ben's brothers." I gave him one of the pictures.

"Look closely," he said. "These are three different people."

I looked closely to find they were different people. After several comparisons, I gave him a picture of Ben's brothers.

"We know this guy. We know he deals with drugs. Can you take us to where you used to meet him?"

"Sure, but he may not be in that area anymore since the write-up about me in this morning's newspaper got out."

"We'll have to take our chances. I just want to know where the spot and houses are located. The other two men are his brothers. They also deal in drugs." He checked me out. We left. He didn't place any handcuffs on me this time.

I took him to about five different locations where we had dealings. Sgt. Jerone got out each time. He looked around, took some notes. I was returned to the county jail. I got back just in time for dinner. Knowing what I know about jail food, I passed. During the course of the day, I was told the food was prepared two days in advance. This was because if there was an up rise in the jail, all the inmates working in the cookhouse would be on lock down. I went up to my cell to lay down while everyone ate.

When chow was over, I returned to the sitting room to watch Television. It was nearing 5 p.m. An announcement came over the intercom saying that I had a visitor. I figure it might be Jane. I had to ask one of the inmates how to get to the visiting area. He pointed to a door between the glass enclosure and cell number one on the ground level. Someone in the glass enclosure pressed an electric switch opening the door. I walked in. The door closed behind me. I walked pass several small booths with stools facing a Plexiglas wall separating the inmates from the visitors. There was Jane sitting in number six's booth. I sat on a stool facing her. We both picked up the phones hanging on the side of the booth. She looked a little sad, but no tears appeared. An officer walked back and forth on her side.

"How's the kids?" I asked.

"They are doing fine. Bill's worried about you. He also wants to know who those men were standing outside yesterday. I told him as much as I thought he would understand. I saw today's newspaper. I'll never buy that paper again. They would have to put it on the front page."

"Yeah. I know a lot of people were surprised to see that."

"My father said he would lend you the money to get out if you needed it. That's unusual for him to do that. You know how he hates to let money go. And speaking of money, I couldn't get any from the bank without your signature. I gave the forms to the officer at the desk. He said he would have someone bring them to you while I'm still here." Just then, an officer walked up behind me carrying the forms for me to sign. I did and gave them back. He left immediately left.

"When you go to the bank, tell them you want to withdraw $10,000. When you get it, pay the lawyer and hold the rest for bail."

"Is there anything I can do or get for you?"

"No. I'll be okay. I should be getting out Monday or Tuesday. Try not to worry about me. O.K.?"

"O.K."

"I'm not going to work on Monday. So, call down here as soon as you find out something."

"I think you should be going. I know you don't like to see me like this." I could see she was holding back the tears. She stood up. Then walked out of my sight. I went back to the cell block area.

I watched the news until 7 p.m. There was no mention of me. I called Bill to see how he was doing. He hold me about his new tape he had bought that day and some of the other things he did. I told him to obey his mother and that he was a good boy. I also spoke with my other son Sam. He didn't talk much. He wanted to know what I was doing and when was I coming home. All I could tell him was soon. I asked him was there anything important he wanted to tell me. His reply was no. I told him I had to go. We hung up. I went up to my cell to lay down. Shortly after I got there, Smith came to see me.

"What happened with you?" He asked.

"I got caught up in the drug action at the prison. I'll tell you more about it when I get out. I don't know if this cell is wired up."

"Is there anything I can do for you?"

"No. Not really."

"If I get a chance tomorrow, I'll come check on you."

"That sounds good."

"I'll see you later."

"Later." He walked out of sight. I heard the electric door open and close.

I looked around in the cell. There was nothing to do. I got up from my bed and went to look out the small window for at least twenty minutes. It was dark outside by now. Night had fallen. The streets were lighted. There were a few cars moving up and down the freeway. A couple was walking along the side of a large parking lot. One of them was pushing a baby carriage. I looked up toward the sky. There were only a few stars shining through the clear sky. For the first time, I had been relieved from the depression of being in jail. But for now, as I was walking away from the window and out of my cell to go watch television, it was all coming back. One thing I had in my favor. There were others here with similar problems.

I found a good location. I took a seat. The men at the table had been here most of the day in the same spot. They were still talking about how they were able to get drugs. Who they sold them to and what they did with the money they made. They talked about women who did stupid things and the adventures associated with them. I listened off and on while watching television. By now, the time was approaching 11:30 p.m. and everyone was told to return to their cell. Everyone got up and did so. As I lay on my bed still fully clothed, once again I started hearing cell doors closing. This time I didn't get a feeling of claustrophobia.

I pulled the sheet over me. Soon I drifted off to sleep. Day two had ended.

I woke up a short time later. My blood pressure was starting to rise. I could feel my body starting to overheat. I got up, went to the sink. Turned on the cold water and started splashing it in my face. In a short period of time, I was coming back to normal. This time I took off my clothes. Then got back into bed. Pulled the blanket over me and drifted off to sleep.

I was awaken by the lights coming on. I must have stayed awake for only a few minutes. I drifted back to sleep. I was again awakened. This time it was from the sound of cell doors opening. I was having problems staying asleep but I was determined not to get too upset because this was a temporary thing.

An officer called over the intercom for everyone to come for breakfast. I didn't move. An inmate came to my cell with my breakfast on a tray.

"Do you want your food this morning?"

"No. Not this morning."

"Can I have it?"

"Yeah. It's yours."

"The officer told me I have to offer it to you."

"I understand. No Problem. Take it and go."

He walked out of sight. Another inmate came running up to my cell.

"You told me I could have your food."

"I don't care who gets it. I don't want it. You'll have to talk to the dude with the food." He left. I could hear him telling the other inmate to give him half. I didn't hear another word about it.

I was fully awake by now. I got up. Washed my face and brushed my teeth. I put on my clothes. By now, the inmates had finished eating. I went down stairs to join them sitting around a table. The inmates were playing cards.

"You haven't eaten anything since you've been here have you?" Asked one of the inmates who had been watching me and my moves since I been here.

"No. I haven't eaten since Thursday and today is Sunday."

"You going to get sick if you don't eat."

"I'm 28 pounds overweight. I think I can make it until tomorrow or Tuesday." He went back to doing something with his cards. Since it was Sunday, no activities were taking place. I spent the whole day divided among talking, watching television and sleeping off and on. At 7 p.m. I called home. Jane picked up the phone. The operator asked if she would accept a collect call. She agreed. The operator connected us.

"Jack, you wouldn't believe how this phone has been ringing off the hook all day. Friends who read the paper called wanting to know if they could help. I thought that was nice of them. No one in your family called or came around except your brother Roger. He was stone drunk but at least he called. I'm going to get on the rest of them. They could at least called to see how I was doing, or if I needed anything. Your mother didn't even call. My mother and father did come to see if they could be of some help. They are here now. Some of your people's friends called asking me to return their checks. I told them no. Then I tore them up and put them in the garbage. There were four of them. Check this out. Your-ex-wife called. She said I should have believed her when she told me you were no good. She's telling everyone she knows about you getting in trouble. I hung up on her. I don't need that type of noise from anyone at a time like this."

I didn't like the idea of Jane throwing money away. She did what she thought was best. Surprisingly, I was glad to see I still had some friends. About my family, they are wrong, but that's the way they are. If they can't help you, they won't make any further problems.

"How's Bill and Sam?"

"Bill misses you. Sam is just like you. He won't say how he feels. But on and on, everyone is doing okay. My father was going to take Bill out to buy him a sandwich but he said he wanted to be here at 7 o'clock when you call. Let me put him on the phone."

"Hi Dad. When you coming home?"

"In a couple of days."

"Dad. Mom bought me a new game today. I can play it good. It's the same type they have at the Mall with the race track."

"Maybe you can show me how to play it when I get home."

"O.K. Do you want to speak to Mommy again?"

"No."

"Bye Dad."

"Ask Sam if he wants to speak to me." Bill was calling Sam loudly with his mouth still to the receiver. I could hear Sam saying. "No."

"Sam said no."

"O.K. Good bye Bill." I hung up and went back to my seat.

Eleven thirty came quickly. The day had ended. The television was turned off. We returned to our cells. We were again locked in. A couple of guys who were holding a heavy conversation while we were sitting at the table didn't let night or being locked in stop them from talking. They continued to talk well into the night. I drifted off to sleep. Sometime later I woke up. It was still dark. By this time other inmates had joined in on the conversation. They had gotten so excited and loud that an officer came from behind the glass booth into the cell area. He had told them to be quiet or consider themselves on report. They lowered their voice and continued talking. I went back to sleep.

CHAPTER FIFTEEN

Jane was up early this Monday morning and rushed the kids off to school. Then returned home to watch television until the bank opened. There were only a few people in the bank when she arrived. Within thirty minutes she had the bank account processed and money in her hands. Then proceeded immediately to the lawyer's office. At first she couldn't find a parking space. She drove around the block several times before being able to find one. After getting out of the car, she had to walk up several steps to the front door. The lawyer's office was located on the first floor. She turned the door knob and walked down a narrow hallway to the rear end where on the door was the lawyer's name. She walked up to the Receptionist's desk. Gave her name and immediately took a seat until it was her turn to see him. A short time later, the lawyer came out and called her in. He took a seat behind his desk while she took a seat facing him.

"Is your husband still in jail," he asked.

"Yes. He's been there the whole weekend."

"Do you have the $2,500?"

"Yes. Here it is."

She reached into her pocketbook. While talking to him. Pulled out an envelope and handed it to him. "Will you be able to get him out today?"

TRAPPED BY IMPULSION

"I don't know. I'll have to see the judge to get his bail reduced. But first I'll have to find out just what exactly he is charged with. Is there anything you can tell me about what happened?"

"No. Not really. Except the police came around 8 a.m. Jack let them in. All of them were in the dining room. The children and I was in the bedroom. One officer came into my bedroom. He told me to take the kids and leave. We did. That's all I can tell you."

"O.K. I'll go see him immediately after we finish. On your way out, stop at the receptionist's desk. Pick up your receipt for this money. If that's all, I'll be getting in contact with you."

"Thank you."

"Have a nice day."

She rose from her seat and walked straight to the receptionist's desk. The receptionist was talking on the phone with the lawyer and looking in a side draw for her receipt book. After locating it, quickly she wrote down a phone number. Then made out a receipt and handed it to Jane. Jane looked it over and left.

The Lawyer finished up some of his unfinished business. Then went to his car and headed toward the courthouse. He went immediately to the judge's chamber. They made arrangements for me to have another bail hearing tomorrow. Then he came to the jail to inform me of what was to take place tomorrow. All I could do was to agree. Just before he left, he told me to make it through the day. I would be out tomorrow. We shook hands.   He left without further comment. I went back to my cell.

By now, the effect on me not eating was taking a toll on my stomach. I started to get small hunger pains. I went up to my cell and drank a cup of water. This was the first of anything I had since Thursday morning. I laid on my bed thinking. All there is to do around here is eat, sleep and watch television. What a waste of life.

About a half hour later, Sgt. Jerone came to visit me. We talked in a small booth for a while. Then he checked me out. We rode to the police station. There he showed me more pictures and asked me more questions. Some I could answer. Others, I didn't know anything about. Then he took me to some locations here in town that Ben's brother was known to have been hanging out. Since I don't really hang out. I didn't know the people or their activities. Without any luck on his part, we returned to the jail.

There were three guys sitting at the table I always sit at. They were talking about prison people in general. I began to think about their discussions. One guy was saying, "I used to be a nice kind-hearted person. I had respect for the people around me, my family and the law. Over the years, I mean from the time I was fifteen up until now and I'm 38, a lot has happened to me to make me dislike a lot of people and things. During this period I went from being nice to mean. Take for example, my friends. At one point I would give them the shirt off my back. All they had to do was ask for it. Then they started using me for dumb stuff. I started getting on to them. When I questioned them about it, they lied to me. I lost faith in them. I had to start thinking about doing some things and not doing other things like loaning them stuff and money. My family was even worse. My brother used to take. Not borrow, but take my clothes. At first I use to say okay. If you were going out, you needed it, sure. Brothers can share. Then it got to a point where they were wearing my stuff because it looked better on them then it did on me. They would even borrow money and not return it. I started getting smart. But not fast enough. My friends and brothers started stealing stuff too. They got me in on it. Man, I was really stupid. We used to go into big department stores and walk out with two and three sets of clothing on. The first time I got caught stealing, the police beat me with their night sticks saying let this be a lesson to not steal. I got mad and developed a hatred for them every since. It wasn't just me. They were beating every person they thought they could get away with. And even today, some of them think because they wear a badge, they consider themselves above the law. They can hit and assault you.

But if you do it to them, be prepared to do some time or they might kill you. I was afraid to go to jail the first time. I had heard how bad it was and what other inmates would do to you. When I got there, it was totally different. You can be a fag if you want to. But if you got heart, ain't nobody gonna bother you. Every now and then you might have to bust one of the tuff guys in the head to let them know where you stand. The other inmates would back off. In fact, some of them will even look up to you. When I got older, I started going to prisons a lot. Guys like me would come and go all the time. The lazy ones liked it. They'll come in for a year. Stay out for six months and go back again. Some of them don't even stay out six months on the street. In here, you didn't have to work. We get fed three squares a day. Given a place to sleep and they even gave us money and health and comfort items. And most of us don't have to stay in our cell all day.

You can watch television from 8 a.m. to 12 midnight on some days. You can go out in the yard a couple hours almost every day. You buy snacks to eat while you play your radio as loud as you want to. Some guys think this is the greatest thing going. So, when someone mentions to them about going to jail, they laugh in their faces. Most of these guys have more friends in jail then out on the streets. In recent years, I've begun to feel the same way. I know over half the guys in here. I can bet you any amount of money you want to bet that when and if I come back here the next time, half of the guys I know in here now will have gotten out and returned. Most of them are not in here for committing serious crimes. It's petty stuff that keeps them coming back. If you ask a guy about going home, he might tell you he can't wait to get out of here. But as soon as he's on the streets, he comes straight back to his old stomping grounds to hook up with his old friends from doing the same things that got them in here in the first place."

I left the table to call Bill. It was 7 p.m. The phone rang and rang and rang. They must have made Bill go out with them. Otherwise, he would be the first to answer the phone. Since I should be going home tomorrow, I won't call again tonight. I watched television until ten. Then I went up to my cell and went to bed. I slept the whole night without waking up.

8 a.m.

I was awakened by an inmate offering me breakfast. As usual I refused. I was also tired of them asking me to eat food I had no desire for. I got up and washed up. I was called down to the glass booth. My cell door was already opened. I went down to see what was happening. By this time they had called six other inmates also. An officer took all of us down to the first floor to the nurse's office. I wasn't moving too fast. I had started feeling weak this morning when I got out of bed. One by one, the doctor was calling us in for a physical. We were told to take off all our clothes and wrap a towel around our waist. We all complied. I was the last one to be called. First I was weighed. I had discovered that over the past few days of being here, I had lost 12 pounds. I told them I couldn't eat their food because it was unfit for human consumption. The staff made no comment as usual. Next I was required to give a urine sample. I did so. They took my pulse. Fine. Then came the hard part.

"We want to take your blood," said the doctor.

"No you won't. You doctors are using the same needles over and over. You're just changing the blood tubes. With AIDS going around, I'm not taking any chances."

"Well. We want it because it's required."

"I'm not giving it. You gonna have to take it against my will."

They called the shift Captain into the room. "What's the problem?"

"This man won't give blood."

The Captain took on a mean composure. "I'll get it. Come here. I'm taking your blood."

"I'm not coming anywhere. And that's what you'll have to do." I didn't move. The Captain didn't move.

"Officer." Speaking to the one who brought me down here. "When you take this man back to his cell area, have him locked in until he cooperates."

I had made a hit with the other inmates. I had stood up to the authorities and they backed down. I did what I thought was right and I was willing to go the distance for it. Even to lockup.

We entered the cell block area. I was escorted to my cell. I entered and the officer signaled the officer in the glass booth to lock me in. The door closed leaving me inside. I really didn't care. I figured my lawyer was getting me out soon.

10 a.m.

I was called to the glass booth. My lawyer had come with Sgt. Jerone to take me to court. We caught the elevator down to the basement and walked to the courtroom. I was told to sit in the front row close to the judge's bench. The judge came in. We were told to rise. He sat. We sat. My lawyer and the prosecutor walked up to the bench. They said something to the judge out of my hearing range. Then both handed him some papers. My lawyer made a small statement followed by a statement from the prosecutor. Without any interruptions, the prosecutor asked that the bail be dropped from $50,000 cash to $10,000 with ten percent bail for release. The judge looked in the direction of my lawyer. He agreed. "So be it," said the judge.

My lawyer and Sgt. Jerone escorted me out of the courtroom to a holding cell. The both of them agreed that one of them would call Jane to inform her I could be let out on bail as soon as she came up with the money and the judge signed his part of a statement. I was finally taken to my cell where I waited until Jane arrived to take me out. I began to feel better.

Three hours later, an officer came up to my cell. I was lying on my back resting. He told me to pack my stuff. I was being released on bail. I complied. Within three minutes, I had all my stuff together and was on my way out of my cell. I was taken to the glass booth where I turned in my bedding. The officer inside instructed me on how to get out of the building. I was free to go. The metal sliding door opened. I following the instructions leading to the back of the building. The judge who set my bail was also leaving out the same exit. He was walking slightly ahead of me. As I was following him, I noticed him fixing his coat over his body. A pistol was strapped to one side of his waist. I thought to myself *'He needs it with all these lose nuts running around in this town'*.

Jane was standing out front. I walked up to her. She led me to her car. She get into the driver's side and unlocked my side from the inside. I got in and she started the car and drive away.

"How did they treat you?" She asked.

"O.K. The food was so bad, I haven't eaten since I was taken there."

"Do you want something to eat?"

"I want some potato chips and ice cream to get my system going again."

She smiled. "You sure do have weird eating habits."

We stopped at the next store.

She went in and soon returned with the items I requested while I waited in the car.

We continued on our way toward home.

"I had my phone number changed," she said. "I got tired of your ex-wife and friends calling. The phone rang day and night. I couldn't get any rest or sleep at night." She pulled into the driveway. We got out and enter the house. "Bill can't wait to see you and I know Sam can't wait either, but he won't show it." See was saying.

"Yeah. Sam is starting to act different. He's starting to get quieter. I don't understand why he doesn't express his feelings. While she talked, I ate the potato chip and ice cream. It only took thirty five minutes to run through my system. Now I was ready for a steak dinner. But first, a nice long shower was in order. I got into the shower, lathered up and stayed a long time until the water started running cold. I got out and dried off. Bill came running into the bedroom. By now I had my trousers on. He jumped on me as a way of showing how glad he was to see me. Sam ran over to hug my waist. I told them how glad I was to be home with them and how I missed them. They left me and went into their bedroom the change clothes. I knew that by day's end, we would be our old family again.

Time passed slowly. During the week I had visited my lawyer once. A State Police Officer had visited my home twice. Once to get my hand writing sample. The other for me to do some undercover work pertaining to a pick up. I told the officer I had to speak with my lawyer before making any type of move like that. He said okay and be careful, but don't ever get back in contact with me concerning this matter. I hung around the house for several days cutting grass, working in the yard and making necessary home repairs. Then it was time to go job hunting. First I applied for unemployment compensation. I was given a hard time. They said I caused my job separation by committing the crime I did. I applied for a hearing. I was told when to appear. In the meantime, I started looking for work. Five out of five places turned me down when I tried to be honest in telling them what had happened at the prison. I decided honesty wasn't the best policy in finding a job. I extended the length of my prior job and added self-employment to my resume. It looked good. When I applied for the next job. I was hired right on the spot. My past would have to remain a secret until I received the findings of my trail. The job was at a supermarket located twenty-two miles away from my home. It was another bakery job.

I adjusted well into the work force. The manager liked me so well, he offered me overtime. I accepted because I needed the money to put on bills.

Several weeks passed. I received notice to appear for my hearing at the unemployment office. I won my case. All my back checks were sent to me. The prison figured out they still owed me money from my vacation and sick time. They sent me a check. Now I was in good shape again. For the next seven months, I continued to make good progress on my job. I was promised a bakery manager's position when a new store, now, in the process of being built and completed in the next several months North of where I lived.

I kept a low profile as directed by my lawyer. At times I thought I was being followed. I stayed as far away as possible from the people who I used to deal with. Sometimes I wondered what the outcome of all this mess would come to if I hadn't been stopped by the law enforcement people. How my lawyer was saying I was getting off light probably facing a fine plus a little jail time. I would read news articles on other drug cases to try to compare their case to mine. Whatever the judge gave them, I could figure I would get close to the same thing. My lawyer told me to try to keep my mind off the case. I would go months without seeing him. I figured he knew what was best. He told me to go out into the community and do some voluntary work. First I worked with a kid's soccer teams, than for a basketball team. When to seasons for both ended, I ask each coach if they could write a letter saying I was working in the community helping kids. They were surprised when I told them the reason for the letters.

The police stopped bothering me after the third week. They must have finished their job with me or found out that I was serving the community in helping kids with sports.

Another four months passed. I was made manager of the new bakery. Still no one knew my charges. Then it happened. The prosecutor sent me a letter through my lawyer that he was interested in the three of us talking about my case. On the day I got the letter, I decided to go to work early the next morning in order to get off in time to see my lawyer.

"Your case is scheduled for hearing in five weeks," he said. "There are several things we have to go over. But we'll talk about them next week just before we visit the prosecutor."

"Okay. I'll do whatever you think is best."

"How is everything else going?"

"I'm working and I'm staying out of trouble."

"Both of them are important. I'll send you a letter letting you know when we should see the prosecutor."

We talked for a little while longer. Then I left.

Before, time was flying by with things happening so fast, now, time was starting to slow down. My problem was also starting to take a toll on my family. It seemed like everyone had fallen into a rut. I decided to start doing more things with them. On a couple occasions, I took the kids to the park. At another time, we went to the movies. Then to the beach and numerous other places after that. Finally, I had Jane take them to Disney World in Florida. I wasn't allowed to go. My travel was limited to this state only.

Three weeks before the trial, I was informed by my lawyer through his letter to report to the prosecutor's office. I complied. The meeting was held on the second floor near the prosecutor's office. My lawyer and I showed up at the same time. The prosecutor directed us to our seats. He sat behind a long desk opposite to us.

"I want you to tell me about the operation at the prison," he said. I told him all about how I brought the marijuana into the prison and how it was passed off to the inmates.

"Can you give me any names of officers or people you dealt with?"

"No officer were involved. The police have a clear picture of one of the main men I picked stuff up from." I went on to explain how I received payment and what I did with the money I received. When I was finished, my lawyer explained to him that I was cooperating with all parties concerned. The prosecutor agreed. He said I didn't look like the type of person who would get involved in this type of trouble. He set up an appointment for me to see a crime case manager. This meeting was over. I was free to go. My lawyer stayed to continue talking with him.

The following week, I reported to the crime manager's office as scheduled with a stack of papers I had been collecting on my case. The receptionist had me take a seat until he was available. Fifteen minutes later, a young looking gentleman came out of an office wearing a dark suit. I was the only person waiting. He walked toward the receptionist's desk. They passed words back and forth. He came to me. "Mr. Wilson?"

"Yes."

"Please follow me." I left my seat and followed him into his office. "Be seated." He said while taking a sat behind a desk to face me. "Do you understand why you are here?"

"Not really."

"My job is to make an evaluation of your present status in this case. I need a list of all your present expenses. Do you have one?" I took all the papers out of an envelope I was carrying. I sifted through the papers until I came up with the list. I handed it to him. "With the type of expenses you have, I assume your wife works?"

"She does." We talked for almost one hour while I explained the various answers to questions he asked. He Took notes of almost everything that was said.

"I'm going to have this typed and a copy will be sent to the judge as soon as possible."

I thanked him for offering to recommend a fine instead of time in jail. He walked me to the doorway. I went straight to my lawyer's office to tell him what I had told the investigator. I also felt I should have given him a copy of the papers I left at the crime manager's office.

CHAPTER SIXTEEN

The day of the trial had come. That morning I got up just after midnight to go to work. Being that I was the bakery manager, I had to make sure the work was well under way before I left. We had a lot of work planned for today and I couldn't afford to miss the whole day. So I worked until 7:30 a.m. About that time, I told my workers and the store manager that it was of the utmost importance that I have the rest of the day off. He didn't like it but he approved it.

Traffic was heavy going back. I drove fifty-five miles to my home. It took nearly two hours. I hurried to take a shower and changed into my medium-brown-colored suit. Off I went toward the courthouse. By now it was nearly 9:50. I was running late. I entered the courthouse. Got directions to courtroom C. Court had not started. I felt relieved. In fact, a court attendant was standing outside the door preventing anyone from entering. I took a seat on a bench facing the door on the opposite side of the hallway. My lawyer approached me from a side stairway.

"Are you ready to go?" He asked.

"Yes. I guess so."

"I'm going to have a talk with the judge. When the prosecutor comes in, tell him to come into the judge's chamber."

I shook my head in response.

The hallway was starting to fill up with people waiting to go into courtroom C. The prosecutor came in. I told him what my lawyer said. He walked off in that direction.

At the far end of the hallway, a couple of officers came in with six men in army work clothes. They were handcuffed to each other. The court attendant asked everyone to move back twenty feet so we would not be in the way of the prisoners entering the same courtroom. They entered first. Immediately afterwards, the attendant asked everyone to line up at the door. One by one he used a hand-held metal detector to check over our body. Afterwards, we went in and took our seat. I sat near the back of the room. My lawyer came in through a side door with the prosecutor. He came straight to me. I was handed several sheets of paper which I was told to read and sign. I did while he waited and I handed them back to him. He said a few words to me. Then he took a seat next to me and we sat in silence.

The judge entered. All rose. He took his seat. Everyone did the same.

"State vs Wilson" was announced by the court attendant. My lawyer approached the bench. I followed. The judge looked at me for a few seconds. Then moved some papers around in front of him.

The prosecutor, who had several papers in his hand, started ready off the charges. "The charges are as follows: Count I: Within the jurisdiction of this court, unlawfully did possess a controlled dangerous substance, to wit: Marijuana. Count II: Within the jurisdiction of this court, unlawfully did possess, with intent to distribute, a controlled dangerous substance, to wit: marijuana. Count III: Within the jurisdiction of this court, unlawfully did distribute a controlled dangerous substance, to wit: Marijuana. Statement of probable cause: The defendant did distribute a quantity of controlled dangerous substance to an undercover State Trooper."

The judge asked. "How do you plead?"

"Guilty Your Honor," I responded.

"Are you aware of all your rights?"

"He is," said my lawyer.

"Proceed with the defense."

"Your Honor," said my lawyer. "My client got involved in a situation through sheer trickery. It was totally beyond his knowledge that drugs were being passed off through him. He became afraid for his family and his life. This is why he continued to handle drugs until the authorities brought his operation to an end. He is a credit to his community. He is an assistant coach for children's soccer and baseball teams. He's on the neighborhood watch group. He's a man with a family. He has no prior police record. When he lost his job last year at the prison because of his involvement, he was able to quickly obtain a job paying almost equal to his prior job. This man has violated the law. But he doesn't deserve to be imprisoned. His family needs his support. Here are three letters, one from the crime management's office. The other two are from team sport coaches. And he has spent time talking with a psychiatrist. The crime manager also aggress that my client should not be imprisoned. His psychiatrist, which he sought on his own because the mental stressing this ordeal has overpowered him, says on the psychiatrist report that Wilson is basically a good person. Imprisonment would only make his life worse. Your Honor, it is inevitable that Mr. Wilson is not likely to commit this crime again. He will never be able to get employment at the prison again."

"Is the prosecutor ready?" asked the judge.

"Yes your Honor. The accused, Mr. Wilson, has indeed committed a crime against the State. He may have been tricked into the drug world. However, he did participate for a profit. He could have sought help in finding an out. He chose to continue to be involved. It is my recommendation that Mr. Wilson be sentenced for a term in prison plus the maximum fine."

"Mr. Wilson, do you wish to make a statement before I impose sentencing?"

"Yes your Honor. I'm sorry I allowed myself to get involved. I tried to get out without losing my employment. In reality, no one got hurt. I'm not the type of person to get involved with drugs." The room was silent. The judge looked over some of the papers again in front of him. Then he spoke.

"I fine you $1,000 for each count. I sentence you to three years of probation. You are to report to the County Probation Office after this court is over. And as a deterrent to future crime, I sentence you to 40 days in the County Correction Facility."

"Your Honor." My lawyer was quick to say. "I believe we discussed a work release program for Mr. Wilson."

"Yes I do believe so. I'm giving you 20 weekends from 7 p.m. on Friday until 10 p.m. on Sunday."

"My client works on the weekend."

"Mr. Wilson. When can you give me two days a week?"

"Your Honor. I only have off on Tuesdays."

"You'll have to find another day to give me. So what days will it be?"

"It'll have to be Tuesdays and Wednesdays."

"On Monday at 7 p.m. you are to report to the County Correction Facility. You will remain there until 10 p.m. on Wednesday. If for some reason you are unable to be there on these days, you are to consult me. I will make arrangements to adjust your situation. Take these papers to the probation office."

A court attendant took the papers from him. He handed them to me. My lawyer led me out of the courtroom. While the next case was being called.

"The State vs Hopkins."

There were a few people in the hallway. Most of them sat on benches and others stood talking in pairs. My lawyer looked at me and said, "I would have liked to have gotten you off without any jail time.

But you know how it goes. I did the best I could. I still consider you to be lucky in getting what you received."

"I really appreciate what you did for me." I shook his hand. He smiled at me. "If I find someone who needs a good lawyer, I'll be glad to give them your name."

"Thank you. Give me a call in a couple of weeks to let me know how you are making out."

"I'll do that." We walked away. I went in one direction. He in another.

I drove directly to the probation office as instructed. It was on the same street about a mile away. I parked in an alley alongside the building. It was a three-story, red-brick type. There were a lot of steps leading up to the front door. I made my way up and walked in. A receptionist sat off to one side of the hallway. I walked toward her looking for directions. She looked up from her typing without speaking to point me in the right direction. As I rounded the corner approaching the office, I could see lots of people standing and sitting near a doorway. I walked in to check with the receptionist. There were four people in line. I got in behind the last person to wait my turn. As I stood, I took notice of the people standing all around inside this office. Most of them were minorities. Some of them looked as though they were on drugs. And others looked like they had stayed up all night. "Waldo," I heard a voice calling out. Waldo went into a small office that had no door. In a loud voice, everyone outside of the office could hear a lady talking to him. "Your cocaine count is higher this week then it was last week. What's happening with you?"

"That's not my test. You must have the bottles mixed up. I ain't had no cocaine in at least one month."

"This is yours okay. These tests don't lie. We do one test at a time. I don't know what we're going to do with you. You've been to the Rehab. Center twice. I think we might have to put you in jail to break your habit."

"No! I tell you I'm clean."

"I'm making this your last chance. If you come back here next week and your cocaine count is equal or higher than this week's, I'm going to call them in to get you. Do you understand what I just said?"

"I promise everything will be better from now on."

"Can you pay anything on your fine today?"

"I have $15 to my name."

"You're supposed to be paying 25. I'll take the 15 but you better come up with an extra 10 on next month's reporting date.

"If I give you my last, what am I going to have?"

"You should have thought about that before you came here or did what you did to wind up here. Do you want to work your fine off in the work house?"

"No."

"You better get on the ball and get your act together. You got two things to work on. Your drug problem and your fine. Now get out of my office."

He walked out of the office talking to himself so everyone could hear him. "I might be better off in jail. I wouldn't have to put up with her. Besides, I could be with my old friends."

I sat waiting my turn and thinking of how hard this lady was on people. A short time later my turn came and she called me in. I handed the papers to her, the ones the judge gave me. She looked over my papers. Then looked up to see my face. "With this charge, they should have dismissed it. But since you're here, Willie will be your counselor. I don't handle these. He has someone in him booth right now. You'll have to wait your turn." She wrote my name down on a yellow sheet under a list of existing names. As I walked back to my seat, Willie walked out of his booth with a client. He was smiling and shaking his hand. "Praised the Lord I can see you're doing a lot better. I'll see you next month." The client walked away never saying a word. He called the next two names. Neither of them answered up. He walked into the lady's office, came out staring at the yellow sheet. For some unknown reason, he called my name.

"Wilson here," I answered up. Together we walked into his booth.

"My name is Willie. Have a seat." I sat in front of his desk while he walked around it and took his seat. His desk was cluttered with papers and figurines. "This had been one busy day. They ought to hold these reporting days at least twice a week."

"Yeah. There sure is a crowd here today. There're people all out in the office and lined along both sides of the hallway."

He looked through a loose leaf note book. "We're going to open a page on you. Are you presently working?"

"Yes."

"Is this your address and telephone number?"

"Yes."

"I see your fine is $3,000." He paused while he continued to read pieces of the papers I gave to him. "And your probation runs for three years. You don't look like the type of person who would get into this kind of trouble."

"Believe me, I'm not."

"As soon as you pay off your fine, you can end your probation."

"I can pay it off in a few months if it's okay with you."

"I'll take that back. You report here for a year. If your fine is paid off by then, than you won't have to report anymore. How much can you pay today?"

"I can't pay anything. I came straight here from the courthouse. I didn't bring any money this time, but I can bring two to three hundred each month."

"That's fine with me." He did some figuring. "If you bring $200 a month for the next 15 months you can possibly stop reporting then. Do you have any questions?"

"No."

"Your reporting day will be the second Tuesday of each month." He took a card from his desk draw and wrote something on it. "Here's a card with your reporting date. Be sure to bring this with your payment. If for any reason you get into any type of trouble or have problems that you think I should know about, you call my number. It's here on the back of this card." He flipped it over to show me. "O.K. So when you call my number, I'll be here." He walked with me out of his booth. We shook hands. I walked through the office, down the hallway and out through the front door to my car.

I went home to change clothes. But after I had taken them off, I decided to lay down to get some rest. I drifted off to sleep. A couple of hours later, I was awakened to the sound of Jane, Bill and Sam moving around in the house.

"I'm surprised to see you're here. I thought you might still be in jail even though I was wishing you was out. So, do you have to spend time in jail?"

"Yes and no. I have to spend two days a week for the next six months at the county jail. I also have to pay a $3,000 fine with three years of probation."

"That's not bad. It's better than having to go away for three years.

"I went back to work the next day. Around noon I figured it was a good time to spring the bad news on my boss. I was hoping he might be in a good mood. I walked into his office. He was busy talking with another employee. So I decided to wait outside. A few minutes later, the employee came out. I peeped in. He was alone. I walked in. "Mr. Tee. There's something I want to discuss with you."

"Have a seat." He said.

I did. "Before I started working for you, I got into some trouble. I didn't lie on my application because at that time I never had been convicted of a crime. Well, yesterday I had to go to court for drug dealing. The judge sentenced me to two days a week in jail for the next six month. I'm requesting to have off from work on Tuesdays and

Wednesdays. I know I've been off on Tuesdays only. If I could have gotten the judge to let me go one day a week, you would have never heard about this."

He looked at me totally surprised. "You mean to say you were dealing drugs that was sold to kids?"

"No. It's nothing like that. These drugs were for out of state people who'd dealings are adult to adult."

"They were still drugs. I don't know if I can spare you two days a week. How about if we give it a try for two weeks. If it doesn't work, you'll either have to come back on Wednesdays or quit this job."

"I'll do all I can to keep the operation running smoothly." I got up, then walked out of his office.

That Monday at 6:15 pm. I packed my toilet articles along with an extra set of underwear. I told the wife and kids I would see them on Wednesday. I got in my car and headed for the Detention Center. The center was almost 17 miles from my home. As I approached it from the highway, I saw it on a hill surrounded by trees. At first it looked like a radio station with its tall antennas. But as I drove closer, the trees started thinning out and a high fence with barbed wire became visible. I reached the turnoff leading up the hill. I made the turn and drove up the hill. I parked in their small parking lot. The building looked small. Maybe 300 inmates at the most could be housed here. I walked up a u-shaped slab of concrete without steps while passing a baseball field and basketball court on my left. I walked through a double set of doors leading into the center. The area was small. On my right were about a dozen chairs and a television on the wall. A walkway was located between a glass-enclosed control center and the chairs. Four officers were manning controls. I could see inmates walking around on the other side through the enclosure. I walked up to the glass window.

"I'm supposed to report here a 7 p.m. this evening."

"What for?" said the Lieutenant.

"The judge said for me to report here for the next six months."

"Have a seat. Wait. What's your name?"

"Wilson. Jack Wilson."

"Have a seat." He asked one of the officers to get my papers from the incoming pile. He looked in several different areas. They were nowhere to be found. He hold the Lieutenant.

"Come here." He waved for me to come to the glass without getting out of his chair. "We don't have any papers on you. Come back tomorrow morning."

"I was told by the judge to report here this day."

"I'm the judge here. Get out of here. Go to the courthouse in the morning and find out what happened to your papers."

"Will I get credit for today?"

"Yes."

I was glad to go. I got into my car and went home. When I pulled into the driveway, it seemed like a new day. I went into the house.

"What are you doing back so soon?" Jane asked in a surprised voice.

"They didn't have my paperwork. I have to get it from the courthouse in the morning."

The next morning at 9. I arrived at the courthouse. I had to walk through a metal detector before going to the record room. I was required to empty my pockets and be checked this time by a hand detector. I passed with no problems. The officer gave me directions to the record room. I walked along the hallway until I found the room. It was a large room with a large counter area. I walked up to the counter. A lady was standing behind it writing something. I captured her attention by clearing my throat. I told the lady why I was here. She looked for my papers. She couldn't find them either. She had to go asked someone about them. When she returned, she told me my papers were sent around 8 this morning. I got into my car. I went to eat breakfast. Then I went back to the center. This time, the day shift lieutenant had my papers. I went through the same entering process as downtown.

I was taken to a cell area for new admittances. I was given a cell located on the second tier near the end. I had Number Twelve. This cell block had two tiers, one above the other, both facing the windows. There was a television attached to a wall between the windows about 6 feet above the floor. The second tier catwalk was about seven feet from the window. Inmates used a broom stick to stick through the bars to change channels.

I made up my bed, then laid on it. I looked the cell over. It was small as usual. It looked like the bars were right on top of me. But I figured I could handle these two days a week as a resting period. I could hear the television playing loud and clear. I had a good spot.

An announcement came over the intercom announcing lunchtime. The food was brought to the second tier. I decided I would try lunch. The food was prepared and placed on paper plates. The cook handed me a plate through the bars on the tier's catwalk. It looked fit to eat. I ate it with no problems. Some of the inmates tried to get seconds while talking loud about the same things they talked about everyday. This included people on the streets, girlfriends and who got out of jail last week and was coming back next week. They didn't talk much to newcomers because they had so many returning friends who stayed out on the streets all the time while they were out of jail bringing back news that the inmates inside had missed. But they had a ball with the old ones. I stayed in my cell most of the day except to eat and watch television. Our living area seemed very small. There was bars everywhere. I could feel the claustrophobia coming back. I put a cold face-cloth on my face. I realized there was a pattern to my claustrophobia. Every time I was placed in a close, confined area by myself, the feeling came over me to want more room. At home I could just walk outside and it would go away. But in here, there was no way for me to get more room. This was probably why the feeling get more intense. I knew this wasn't for me, but I would have to deal with it. In the morning when the cell doors were open, I could escape to the catwalk where a larger area was provided. This was an important factor in calming me down.

11:30 p.m.

Everyone had to go into their cell. I was already laying on my bed. My cell door closed. I heard someone on the first level say they can't take this. I knew I couldn't take it either, but for one or two days a week, I would have to hold up. I finally drifted off to sleep. About three hours later, I woke up with a bad case of claustrophobia. It seemed the more cold water I placed on me, the worse it got. I went to the bars and called the officer. A voice from below answered.

"Hey blood. They go back to the center when the lights go out."

I had to make it until day light. I was going home in a few hours. I tried to block the fear out of my mind. Finally, I told myself this is crazy. When I had almost come around by using the cold water, I dried off and laid on my bed. The next thing I knew, I woke up when breakfast was almost over. My cell door was open. I could hear guys arguing about what they were served. This seemed like the start of a normal day. I got dressed and came out onto the walkway. It must have been around 8 a.m. I checked out the meal. Since I didn't eat breakfast, I went back to my cell to clean up. Afterwards, I laid on my bed listening to the television. Sometime later, one of the guys came to my cell asking me if I played cards. I acknowledged I knew a few games. I spent most of the day playing until they let me out at 8 p.m.

CHAPTER SEVENTEEN

For the next two weeks, I worked hard in the store. Business had dropped half a per-cent point. This wasn't good when you're talking about making a gross sales of $800,000 per week. The bakery traveling manager came to visit me while I was at work. I tried to explain to him that the store manager had reduced the bakers working hours by 50 percent, we had to cut back on production. He refused to make comment. I was beginning to wonder what might be his problems. He avoided looking directly at me. It never dawned on me why he was here. He helped with the production until 3 p.m. Then around that time the store manager called him to his office. A few minutes later the store manager called me to his office. I went but still didn't know why. I entered his office.

"Take a seat," he said. "I have been thinking over what we talked about a couple of weeks ago. I can't spare you two days a week. Can you come back on Wednesdays?"

"No. it's not possible."

"I'm going to have to let you go."

"Yeah. I sort of figured that's what was going to happen sooner or later."

"I wish there was something I could do," said the bakery manager. "It's out of my hands. This is between the company and the store manager. I tried to get a person to fill in for one day but it didn't work. I'm sorry."

"Yeah. So am I. I thought you might ask me to convert back to being a worker and let someone else run the bakery operation while I continue to work as a worker. I see you're not interested in making this type of move."

"No. We are not," said the store manager.

"O.K. Gentlemen," I said. "Have a nice day." I walked out of the office heading back to the bakery to gather my stuff. Then I left. When I arrived at home, Jane was surprised to see me.

"You're home early today. How did your day go?"

"It didn't. They fired me because of the court's decision."

"I'm sorry to hear that."

"Yeah, Me too. There goes my income. I guess it is back to the unemployment office."

"Don't worry. You'll find something."

"Tuesday and Wednesdays. I might have to stick with supermarkets until my time is up at the center."

"I wish you could find something with better hours."

"So do I. But for now, I'll have to take want I can find." I went to change out of my work clothes.

The following Monday, I went to the unemployment office. It must have been the worst day of the week. It looking like everyone and his mother was coming here to put in a claim. I must have been somewhere in the forties in line. The line was moving slowly. There were two windows open for new claims. I managed to get to the head of the line after two hours of waiting. I would have thought my claim would have been processed. Instead, I was handed a stack of forms pertaining to information I previously had given. I had to take them off to one side to fill them out. I began to go through the stack. This is going to be a mess I thought.

"Do the easy forms first." Said a guy standing next to me.

"I come here often." I couldn't tell one form from another. "Which forms do you call easy?"

"Let me help you." He took four forms with yes and no columns on them. Then went down the columns quickly marking the appropriate blocks. "I know them by heart. I come here ever years. I only work long enough to collect. Do something to get fired and back here again. It works for me."

"I can see you been doing this a long time. I think I can do the rest. Thanks for the help."

"No problem. If you get stuck, call me."

I was glad to see him go. He was starting to make me nervous. How do he know what questions I wanted checked off? I started going over the papers. I happened to glance up at him as he was leaving. He made a goodbye gesture with his hand as he disappeared through the front door. I finished up the forms. By this time, the line was shorter. Guess some of the people from the first line took their forms and left being they couldn't afford to tie up their whole day waiting in lines. I was about number nine this time in line. I slowly made my way to the front. I moved up to the counter about 30 minutes later. The lady behind the counter took my papers. She began to look through them. After turning over a few sheets, she stopped. "You can't file a claim for unemployment. You stated here you were terminated because you can't work on Tuesdays and Wednesdays."

"That's right. I still worked five days a week. The weekends were considered normal work days. Therefore, I am entitled to those days."

"I'm going to set your case up for a hearing. I feel I can't make a decision in your favor at this time."

I signed a hearing form and left. I knew I was going to have a problem with this. Anyway, I would have to deal with it later.

About a week passed, I went back to my past bakery job to gather some article I had forgot to take when I left. While I was there, several of my past workers and store friends took me off to one side to fill me in on some information they had heard and thought I should know about it. The Store manager did not fire me because of the days I was not able to work. He fired me for several other seasons. One, the week we were setting up the store, he had asked me to stay and work overtime, and I agreed. It just so happened that I worked 96 hours that week and was paid over $2,000 take home. Somehow, the other workers found out about it and the store manager got in trouble from the main office. Two, I was the only black department manager in the store. He had no say so as to who the main office would send to work in his store. In the twenty year he had been a store manager, he had never had a black department manager working for him. Therefore, he didn't like me or want me in his store. And three, every week when I completed my inventory, he would change the numbers to offset my supply of goods on hand. However, in the past, I had received good recommendations from several area bakery managers to be placed in his store. And so, I was sent there.

I started job hunting again. I couldn't wait for my unemployment to come through. There was a fifty-fifty chance I might not get it. I had clipped out several job leads from Sunday's paper. I spent the rest of the week following them up. I didn't get anything positive. The following week, Jane gave me a lead she got from a lady on her job. It was a store that just opened a few months age across the state line. They needed help badly. I called for an appointment. I was told to come in immediately to fill out an application. I drove to the store. It looked like a large store from the outside although it was part of a shopping center. It was odd that this shopping center was out in the country. Very few houses were located around it. The parking lot wasn't too large but it seemed large enough to handle the business for this area. I entered the store, walked up to the customer's service desk and asked for the manager. He was paged. Shortly he appeared. I introduced myself. He did the same. He took me to his office. I filled out and application while he talked with me.

"If you know anything about baking, we need someone with experience. We will offer you $22,000 a year to start if you will accept a job at this store."

"I don't know. I was making more where I worked last."

"If you work out, I could put you in for a raise in 60 days."

"That sounds fair."

"Can you start today or tomorrow?"

"I can't start until this weekend. There are a few things I must clear up first."

"I'll see you then at 6 a.m. You can report directly to the bakery."

I agreed. I walked to the bakery to check out the operation. It appeared to be operating smoothly. I left for home.

During the week, the store had called twice wanting to know if I was willing to start work before Saturday. Jane told them I was out of town and wouldn't return until Friday. All they could do was wait. In the meantime, I continued to spend my 2 days per week in the Detention Center. I was getting adjusted to the center by now. Only during the first week did I have to spend time in a cell. Now I was housed in a bay area which contained 30 inmates. The unit held 24 beds and 6 cots, I was one of six persons who had to sleep on a cot. At first my body became sore. The cot had no back support. In fact, it was made from some type of strong material stretched between two long poles attached to three X-supports. This was all I was given to sleep on. I accepted it because I knew I would be leaving on Wednesday night. Glad to get back into my own bed at home.

Some of the guys off the street I had known for years were locked away in here. We played cards, watched television and joked with one another day in and day out.

That Saturday, I reported for work on time but the store entrance was locked. There were other employees waiting to be let in. "What's the problem?" I asked the group waiting.

"He ain't never on time." Said one of the women. "Sometimes we wait up to 30 minutes to get in."

I made no remark. A red small car pulled into the parking lot. Someone said, "It's about time." The person was identified by one of the employees as the store manager. He came to unlock the door for all to enter. I followed the bunch to the time clock. One of them showed me how to punch it. I walked to the bakery. Another manager had been working all night with a small crew. He was removing rolls from the oven.

"Hi. I am Wilson. I'm scheduled to start working with you this morning."

"I'm Ron. Did you ever work with this type of equipment and pre-molded frozen yeast products?"

"Yeah I have. And I can make and do anything in the bakery. But if it's a certain way you want something done, you'll have to show me."

"That sounds great. You're just the person I need. I don't have time to train people. We need lemon meringue pies. They're on sale for 99 cents with a coupon. Can you make 175 of them for me?"

"Sure. No problem. Just point me in the direction of the ingredients." Together we rounded up everything. I was on my way. At 8 a.m. other bakery employees started coming in. I found out their functions. It looked like a good crew. I worked the whole day without any problems.

On Monday, I received notice to appear at the unemployment office for my hearing which was to take place on Thursday. That Monday evening I reported to the Detention Center. I went through the usual procedure of having my bag and body searched. When I entered the bay area, a guy named Jones greeted me at the gate.

"Did anybody tell you Sal left?"

"No. I thought he still had 24 days to go. When did he get release?"

"He didn't. He just walked away when he was out of the Center working."

"I thought guards were watching him while he was working?"

"No. He walks out of here every day. The guys who work outside don't need to be watched. They're short timers. Who would think that a short timer would just walk away?"

"I guess he had more important things to do that didn't include this place." "Did he get an honorable mention in the newspaper?" I asked.

Suddenly, the inmate started laughing out of control.

For some reason, I saw no humor in his question.

"Yeah. He got a small paragraph on the sixth page of last week's newspaper. The authorities had to inform the public. Oh yeah. Check this out." He moved closer to me so he wouldn't have to talk loud. "Bob didn't go home last weekend. He went to lockup. Somebody brought a package here for someone. This person asked Bob to accept it for him. Bob went out and signed. The package was searched. They found drugs inside. Then they took Bob to the hole. I heard he was going to get street charges."

"I knew he wasn't too bright. This proves it."

"Yeah. I think they're going to bury him this time." There was a moment of silence. "Do you want to play cards?" He asked.

"Okay. But first I want to get my cot and spot together."

I went to do what I had to do. Then I played cards until it was time to turn in.

The next day I had to get G.F. straightened out. He was the God Father of the whole Detention Center. Anything I needed, he could get for a price with jail house money. Cigarettes were the most thing of value. I had been sending him money to purchase food for me from the Commissary. For a small fee, he would keep it locked in his foot locker until I asked for it. The food in the mess hall wasn't always that great. But when it was, it wasn't enough. So, I had to depend on G.F. to get me through the two days if necessary. People coming for their two-day stay weren't issued lockers. At times, I wondered about people stealing other people's stuff. Did they really need it or was it just an impulsive movement to deprive the owner of it? But I knew deep down inside that G.F. and a few other guys were looking out for me. What little items I had was safe.

That Thursday, I got off work early to keep my date with the unemployment officer. I arrived at 9:30 a.m. in time for my appointment. There was no waiting time to be called. The lady handling my case called me into her office. She had me state my case into a tape recorder. When I had finished, she said she was going to send the results of the hearing to me along with a check for my timeout of work if I had any money coming. I went home. When I got there, I checked the mailbox like I usually do, there was a letter in it for me from the prison. I opened it and red the contents. The letter stated that I had been permanently terminated from my job because I had been found guilty of a felony. I put the contents back into the envelope and went into the house for the rest of the evening.

CHAPTER EIGHTEEN

The alarm clock sounded. With my eyes half-closed, I reached for the night stand to turn off the alarm. Not being able to see it with my eyes half closed, I fully opened then and saw was 8:15 a.m. I didn't have to be at work until 9. So I made my way out of the bed and into the bathroom. When I returned to the bedroom, Bill was laying on my side of the bed. Jane was awake and just and looking in my direction. "You going to work later today?" She asked.

"Yeah. I'm working the 9 to 3 shift. We always have shorter hours on Sunday."

"I hope you have a nice day at work." Said Bill.

"I hope so too, Bill. Thank you." I was in a fairly good mood for some reason. Maybe it was because I went to bed early last night. I got fully dressed and went into the kitchen to fix toast and orange juice for my breakfast. Minutes later, I said good-bye and left for work.

I was driving down the Interstate at a speed of roughly 67 miles per hour. My radio was blasting as I was listening to one of my favorite tunes. As I crossed the hill crest, I noticed a police car moving on the opposite side of the grass median. I looked closely to see if the officer was looking in my direction. As I passed it, I saw the rear lights come on as the car slowed down. He drove across the grass median and came onto my lane about a quarter mile behind me. Just in front of me was the State Line. I had always wondered if the police was allowed to follow vehicles across the line. All this time I never slowed down. The police car started catching up to me. The car put on its overhead flashing lights. By now I was almost on the bridge separating the two states. I suddenly got this impulse to speed up by mashing on the gas. My speed increased from 67 to 80 to 95 miles per hour. The police car with its flashing lights pulled up alongside my car.

"Pull over," shouted the officer through his speaker system. I could just barely hear him through my car radio. I speeded up to 100 thinking I could out run him. However, the chase was on. The officer was getting bent out of shape as he continued to follow me. He couldn't find a way to get his car in front of mine to pull me over. I could see he was on the car phone.

"Headquarters. This is car 775. I am in hot pursuit of a car traveling in speed exceeding 95 miles per hour. Hold it. He just increased his speed. The driver must be crazy to be traveling at this high rate of speed."

"What's your 1020?" Came a voice through his radio.

"I have crossed the State Line on the Interstate Highway. Is there any way I can get backup? I got to get this car to pullover."

"We're going to try to radio to the next town to set up a road block."

"Hurry. I'm out of my boundary. How far can I continue to pursue him?"

"Continue until we contact someone."

"10-4."

I looked down at my gas gauge. It was on empty. I looked through the rear view mirror to see a brown unmarked car with its lights on following close behind the police car. We were now about four miles across the State Line and still traveling. I was approaching the turnoff to my job. In a split decision, I took the turn. I had to slow down to nearly 45 miles per hour because I was approaching traffic on a two-lane road. I drove up to the top of the hill. Then slowed down even more at the yield sign. Both cars were still behind me. Suddenly, the brown car sped pass me. I continued driving at 35 miles per hour with the police car directly behind me. The brown car slowed down in front of me bringing me to a dead stop and blocking me in a way to prevent me from moving my car. Cars were now passing us on the opposite lane. I sat in my car with the radio on and the engine running. I noticed ahead that the guy in the brown car had gotten out of his car and was running toward me. I could see a lady in his car. She never moved. The police man was still sitting in his car talking on his radio. Now the man from the brown car had reached my car. He was moving his lips. I couldn't make out what he was saying. He grabbed the handle of my door. Yanked the door open. In a rage of furry, he screamed, "Get out of there!" Before I could move, he reached across my chest and with a thrust so strong, broke out the glass on the dash panel covering the gauges. He pulled his hand back far enough to grab my keys and turned off the engine. Then he looked at me for a split second. Grabbed my shirt. Tore off three buttons as he pulled me out of my car. He caught my left arm and spent me around while twisting it upward. Then pushed me up against the side of my car. I saw the policeman come running from his car with his pistol out. When he reached me, he placed the barrel up against the side of my head. With his other hand, he placed a handcuff around the wrist of my hand that the man was holding and yanked my hand down toward the other where he placed the second cuff onto the lose wrist. "I got you now," he said in an angry voice. I saw him place his pistol back into its holster.

"Why the rough treatment?" I asked with anger in my voice.

"Shut up!" He screamed.

The cuffs on my wrist were clamped on so tight, I began to lose feeling in both my hands. He then pulled me by my arm over to his car. He opened the back door and pushed me inside and locking the door. He went back to my car to join the other man in searching for whatever they could find.

During all this action, people passing by in their vehicles slowed down to look in total amazement at what was happening. I was angry at what was taking place myself. These officers were acting like animals. Running around and screaming. I remained motionless in a half-sitting and half-laying position on the seat. A short time later, the policeman came back to his car. He got in. Called headquarters to inform them he was bringing me in. I saw the man who had the brown car driving my car away. It had been blocking part of the traffic on one side of the road. The policeman started his car and we road down the road toward the state where I had crossed the border into.

The police officer looked through the rear view mirror in my direction.

"You're such a stupid person," he said. "I'm going to break your face when I get you back to the police station. Who do you think you are trying to give me the slip?"

"I don't understand why you're talking violently and so set on doing bodily harm to me. I bet if I was a white guy, you wouldn't be acting like this."

"Shut up. You wait and see. I'm going to break every bone in your body."

"You know I live two blocks from the police station. You do something to me and you'll see me again, soon." He was quiet from that point on.

We arrived at the station. I had been there before when I was picked up on the drug charge. The officer opened the car's back door. Pulled me out by my arm and led me into the station. I was taken downstairs where I was fingerprinted and they took my picture. I was taken to another room where I was charged with evading apprehension and excessive speeding. I was not red my rights. However, I was given a paper to sign pertaining to them. I refused to sign it. Two of the officers on duty at that time, of whom I recognized as part of the team who came to my home as part of the drug raid, looked at me strangely but said nothing.

I broke the silence by saying, "I know you guys have been watching me. I live on a dead-end street. Cars go in and come out on the same end. I've seen the cars parked in my area. Up until last year, I have never seen a police car on my street. Now, sometimes I see them parked near my home and even turning around in my driveway." No one said a word. "My wife told me to go as straight as I possibly. She knows people who you know are saying you guys want me. You was just waiting to get your chance."

One of the officers spoke up. "If you're into crime, yeah, we're onto you."

Another officer came to the desk where the officer was writing up charges on me. He spoke directly to the writer. "I don't understand why he was speeding. There are no warrants out on him. Maybe it's the 18 points on his driver's license that sparked him into crossing the border."

I said nothing. The other officer leaned against the wall. The officer doing the writing stood up and went into another room. A few minutes later, he returned. "How much money do you have?" He asked.

"What's this? A bail stick-up?" Was my reply. "Everybody's asking me about money."

"You got that right if you wanna get out of here today, you'll have to post bail."

"I got $50."

"You just made bail. I'll give you a receipt for that."

"What if I only had $25?"

"Don't be asking questions. Just be lucky you're getting out."

The officer who brought me into the station gave me a hard look. "You better thank your lucky stars you're getting out."

I didn't pay any attention to him. He went to the door and left. I took the money from my wallet and gave it to the officer who was letting me out on bail. In return, he handed me a charge sheet with a date to report to court and a receipt for my money which was attached to the bottom. I was shown the way out. When I reached outside, I started shaking my wrist to restore the feeling.

I walked home from the police station which was a 20 minute walk to get my other car. I was still going to work even though I was close to being 2 hours late. I knocked on the door. Jane opened it on the first ring. "Where have you been? Your boss has been calling. He called twice. I told him you was not at home. On the second call, he said he needed you to decorate a cake for an 11 o'clock pick up. Then he said something about Beth, the counter girl might be able to do it. She could ice cakes and do writing. Maybe she could put a simple border and one or two flowers on it. I don't know why he was telling me all this." She looked at me in a sad way. "I thought something had happened to you." She looked past me. "Where's your car? And why did you ring the doorbell?"

"You ain't going to believe this. I got stopped for speeding. They took my car, money and keys." I entered the house and she closed the door behind me. We stood by the steps.

"Oh Jack. You got to be kidding."

"No. straight up. I think they were looking for drugs."

"Did you have anything in the car or on you?"

"No. You should know better than to believe I was still fooling with drugs after the mess I just went through."

"That's good. I just don't understand why they would take your car?"

"I'll take care of it in due time." We walked up the steps. She went into the kitchen where Bill and Sam were eating. I went into our bedroom to get the extra set of keys to everything. The keys were not where we normally keep them. I had to call her to get them. She gave them to me. I went into the garage to get the car. Then took off toward my job.

When I arrived, it was almost 11:30. The bakery manager was upset about me just arriving for work.

"Where have you been?"

"I...." He cut me short.

"I thought maybe you got into a car accident or something. I called your house twice. Talked to your wife. I told her to have you call me as soon as you came in."

"She didn't tell me that part, but it is okay. I just left home. She knows I'm okay. As to what happened, the police took my car because I was speeding this morning. That's why I'm late."

"Just speeding?"

"Well, it was for a couple of other reasons also. But nothing serious."

"Do you want to talk about it?"

"No. Let it go for now."

"Let's go to work. I need your help." We did just that.

That evening when I got off from work, the first thing I did was to go back to the Police Station to find out where my car was towed. I entered to find the same officer on duty. I walked up to the booth. "Can you tell me where my car is? They took it from me this morning."

"Wait a minute. I'll check." He walked off into a back room. A few minutes later he returned. "We didn't have anything to do with your car. The police from across the State Line took control of it."

"How do I get in contact with them?"

"Here's the address and phone number. This other police station called us and left this information with us."

I took the paper. Got into my car and went to the State Trooper's station across the State Line. When I arrived, they told me my car was at a gas station about 10 miles away. I felt I was being giving the run around. However, I had to follow my leads. When I arrived at the gas station there, I saw my car parked in a fenced-in area. I parked on the side of the station. Got out of my car. Went in to see the attendant. "I would like to pick up my car. It's in the fenced-in area."

"I'm sorry. The person who takes care of the towed cars isn't here right now. As a matter of fact, he won't be back until tomorrow."

"I need my car today." I started to get angry.

"There's nothing I can do about that. You'll have to see him tomorrow."

"How much is it going to cost me to get it back?"

"Well, let me see. It's $75 for towing and $50 a day for storage. There's no storage charge for today. You'll have to pay $50 for tomorrow."

Now I became mad. "I'm not paying that. I want my car now."

He started to get angry. "I'm telling you, you can't get it. If you don't want to pay the $50, that's okay with the yard boss. We'll sell your car to the State Police."

Nothing was working. I left without further conversation. When I got home, I told Jane about the car problem. "As long as you keep those personalized license plates on these cars, you're going to be having continuous problems with the police for quite a while."

"I realized that, but I'm not giving anything up for their satisfaction. And I'm not hiding from them."

"Well, they're going to bother you every chance they get."

"I'll just have to deal with it or get my lawyer to handle it."

"You know what that means? You're going to need money to keep yourself straight."

"You're probably right."

The next day, when I got off from work, (this was Monday), I had to report to the Center by 7 p.m., but first I had to get my car to stop the storage fee. I arrived at the gas station around 1 p.m. I was told to go back to the State Police Headquarters to get a release report. 2 p.m. I arrived to find the officer who wrote the report had the day off. Another officer went to work right away in trying to locate both the officer and the report. About an hour and a half later, the report was located but not the officer. I was given a verbal okay to pick up my car along with a telephone number for the station owner to call for verification. I returned to the station around 4:30, just in time to catch the owner leaving. I gave him the number to call. I paid him. He gave me the keys. Since I was already driving my spare car, I chose to leave the car I was driving there. I drove home to get Jane. By this time it was getting late. I had to take my clothes and toilet articles with me that I was going to need at the Center. I drove Jane to the gas station. We both got out of the car. I could see by looking through the window that the car had been trashed. I was half angry but right now there was nothing I could do. I unlocked the door. Got behind the wheel. I started picking up papers off the floor and seats. I was shocked to find my glasses underneath the papers with both lens broken. Also, I noticed my radio's face was split in half. I started checking the rest of my car for damages. I discovered the wires for my rear window defroster were pulled out and my radar detector wire was cut in half. By now I had passed angry. I was on fire with anger. I called Jane over to the car.

She looked inside. "They did all this?" she asked.

"Yeah, but don't do anything foolish." She went back to her car. Drove off. I got into my car and drove off toward the Center.

For the next two days, I thought about ways to get even with the guy who trashed my car. Then I finally realized that I would only be getting myself into more trouble. I decided I would call my lawyer and let him handle this situation. I made a call to get an appointment to see him. It was arranged for Friday afternoon. I started feeling a little better at this point.

I sat on my cot in the Detention Center watching television. There was a story having something to do with an identity crisis. Jones, one of the inmates was sitting next to me watching as well.

"You know," he said. "That's what's wrong with some of these guys in here. They don't know how to be their own man. They can't exist without trying to imitate someone. I tell them. 'Be yourself. People will respect you more for that.' When the image wears off. You look like a phony. That's when trouble starts brewing. Now check the out. This is just a story right?"

"Right."

"These people make it look so real and they get away with a lot, but in reality, it just don't work like that in real life. You don't see any of these guys in jail. Then again when you do, they get out within 24 hours. These guys in here have problems getting out in 24 days. What I'm trying to say is that these guys are going to have to think more about what they do before they act."

Lunch was called over the intercom. We got up and started walking toward the mess hall. He continued to talk but was partly drowned out by the voices of inmates walking close to us going in the same direction. He moved very close to me and started talking loud.

"Right now, they don't realize that they ain't into nothing except here. Myself, I want to be me. That's what I want to be known as."

"I can understand that."

He walked off toward one of his friends. I continued to go into the mess hall.

This was my last week to spend at the Detention Center. Time had gone by fast and now this part of my sentence was over. It would be nice to let the guys know I was departing for good this week but I remembered what they did to Ted when he told them he was leaving. That night when the lights were turned out. They made him strip down to his waist. They tied him to the bars. One by one, each of his friends took turns hitting him with wet towels. They beat him until he was sore. I know the officers heard him crying out in pain. For some reason, they never came to his rescue. I think they really knew this deal. The next day the inmate left smiling and just barely walking. I don't think I could have handled things the way he did. This was probable his friend's way of saying don't come back.

The next morning after breakfast, I started letting guys know I was leaving. I couldn't hold it in any longer. Some were glad to see I had completed my time. Others acted as if they didn't want me to leave because I was bringing in movie tapes to be played on movie night. This was something different. The inmates enjoyed them.

Some inmates stated they were also leaving within the next few weeks. I told them I wished them a lot of luck on the outside.

It was nearing 10 a.m. I went out to the center to find out what time I would be leaving. I had known on the days when guys were leaving, they were told at 6 p.m. to pack up. I didn't understand why they hadn't called me. The officer in the booth was calling for me upstairs. I was quick to answer up, "Here,"

"Mr. Wilson. They say you can leave now. If you can arrange transportation."

"No problem. I have my own transportation parked outside."

"Good. Pack your stuff."

"Are there any papers for me to sign?"

"No. your time is up. Just go. Tell the officer to call us when you're ready to leave."

I did just that. When I stepped outside the Detention Center, it didn't feel any different. I guess it was because I had been staying only two days a week. Maybe I would feel different next week when I'm at home on the days I was to be spending time here. I got into my car and drove off without ever looking back.

CHAPTER NINETEEN

The following week I was due to appear in court with my lawyer for the traffic violation. The appointment I made with him for Friday was cancelled due to an important case which required his attendance. I made a call to his office. "Hello. I'd like to speak with the lawyer."

She put me on hold for a few minutes. Then came back with, "Yes. Can I ask your name?"

"Mr. Jack Wilson."

"I'll put you through to him right away." There was a moment of silence.

"Hello Jack," came a voice from the other end. "How's things going?"

"O.K. I was calling about my court appearance. Can I come in to see you now? I have a few things to tell you I think you should know."

"O.K. Make it around 3:30 this afternoon. I'll see you then. I'm with a client right now, See you then."

I gathered my notes I had written about the incident that had placed. I checked them over to make sure I hadn't left anything out. I folded the papers into about one quarter of its size and stuffed it into my pocket. Then sat around watching television until it was time to go. At exactly 3:30 I arrived at his office. He was talking with his secretary when I walked it. "You're right on time. Not a minute too soon."

"Yes. This case is important. I'm the victim."

"Come into my office." I walked in and took a seat. "Does it have anything to do with drugs?"

"No. I haven't touched any drug since the raid on my home."

"Tell me about what happened."

I told him the whole story. I didn't take my notes out of my pocket. I figured what I had said to him was enough to cover everything."

"It looks like you have a problem."

"Can I press charges against them for what they did to my car?"

"No. You better let it go. If you do, they'll probably come up with something else to charge against you."

"You know this is not fair."

"Yes. I know. You're lucky it was that Township Police who got you. I can probably get one of the charges dropped. The Judge is a friend of mine and so is the prosecutor. We grew up together. If the arresting officer wants to play it hard, I'll just have to trip him up in the courtroom."

"How much do I owe you for taking my case?"

"I'll let you off cheap with $1,000. You got to stay out of trouble. The charge of evading could cause you to spend your probation time in jail. I don't want to see that happen."

I wrote him a check. He looked it over. Smiled at me. I stood up. Reached across his desk and shook his hand.

"Be at the courthouse next week. I'll meet you there. There won't be any need for me to see you again before then."

"Okay. Thank you." I said and walked out.

The lawyer got on the phone. "May I speak with the prosecutor?" He gave his name. There was a moment of silence. "Hi. Can you meet me for lunch tomorrow?" There was another moment of silence. "Great. If 1:30 is okay, I'll see you then. A moment later, he hung up.

The following week I appeared in court on time. My lawyer hadn't shown up before me. I took a seat in the courtroom and watched different officers walking in and out of the courtroom. I was looking to see if I could recognize the officer who arrested me. No such luck. The judge came in. The court attendant red off the names of persons to have their cases heard. My name was first. I told the attendant my lawyer hadn't arrived. He told me to have him see him when he arrived. It was at 7:30 p.m. when my lawyer appeared. He walked over to me. "Did they call you yet?"

"Yes. I told them you weren't here. The court attendant wants to see you."

"Don't worry about a thing. I talked with the prosecutor. He's only charging you with a speeding ticket. I'll be back. I'm going to see him now." He walked off toward the hallway leading to the judge's chamber. I sat listening to some of the other cases. About 20 minutes later, my lawyer reappeared. "You're next after this case. I'm going to move up front so I can get the Judge's attention after this case." He did just that. I stayed where I was seated. A few minutes later the case ended.

"Your Honor. I'm ready with my defendant."

"Are all parties present?"

"Yes your Honor."

"Mr. Prosecutor are you ready?"

"Yes your honor."

"Will everyone approach the bench?" My Lawyer signaled for me to come forth. "Proceed Mr. Prosecutor."

"Your honor. The defendant's Lawyer and I have reviewed and discuss the case. The charge of evading cannot be proven. It appeared, the defendant was traveling to work at a high rate of speed because he was running late. I requested the charge be dropped. However, I would like for the speeding violation to stand."

"How do you feel about the Prosecutor's decision?" Judge speaking to my Lawyer.

"Your Honor, my client will accept his decision."

"If all parties agree, there is no use in carrying this case any further. The speed was over one hundred miles per hour. It appears you were really in a hurry." He shuffled through some papers on his desk. "The fine will be $155. When can you pay it?"

"You have my bail check. I wish to put that toward my fine. I can pay the rest this Friday."

"Be here before 4:30. If you fail to pay this fine, I'll have to issue a warrant for your arrest. Do you understand what I'm saying?"

"Yes your Honor."

"You can go." We walked out of the courtroom.

"See how easy that was?"

"Yeah. But I know it was more to it than what just took place in the courtroom. I guess it's who you know that counts."

"You're right. The next time it won't be so easy."

"I don't plan on getting into any more trouble."

"Nobody plans it. Most of the time it just happens." We shook hands and went our separate ways.

I remembered that I hadn't gotten a newspaper today. I walked to a coin-operated newspaper box. Put my coins in the provided slot. Pulled the window down. Took out a paper and started walking toward home. I decided to glance at the paper. I was startled. I didn't believe what the headlines was saying. 'STATE PRISON SUPERVISOR NABBED WHILE PASSING OFF DRUGS TO INMATE.' I know how he must feel. It's a shame that another victim was heading down the same road I just got off. I had learned a lot about the drug business in just over two years. The bottom line is, it's a slow, sure way to self-destruction. If you deal with drugs long enough, you'll either get caught selling them or you'll become a user. The profit is lost one way or another, I thought to myself.

I folded the newspaper in half and placed it under my arm as I rounded the corner.

CONTINUATION FROM FRONT COVER

Soon, the money starts rolling in faster than Jack can count. Life seems to take an upswing... until that fateful day when a harsh rapping of policemen's fists is heard at the front door and the Wilson family is cast into a hellish nightmare of pain, heartache, and harassment.

What happens to Jack, the author points out, can happen to anyone, anywhere. But it could also have been avoided, and it is with this sentiment that Charles Feggans has written this compelling and always fascinating novel of drug involvement aimed at telling people how low our life can sink before we are forced to regain control----or lose it forever.

From the psychological attraction of drug abuse and illicit income to the threats posed to future employment, health, and family stability, Mr. Feggans' novel stresses the importance of being your own person, not letting the outside world apply pressure and persuasion that could very easily destroy an entire life.

In this era when drug abuse is at its most rampant, *Trapped By Impulsion* should be read by each and every one of us, for there's a lesson to be learned from it.

ABOUT THE AUTHOR

Charles Feggans was born in Philadelphia, Pennsylvania, and was raised in neighboring Trenton, New Jersey. During his tour of duty in the U.S. Marine Corps, he became a skilled baker, a trade he worked with for more than 35 years while at the time writing this novel. Between work and caring for his wife and three children, he obtained his Bachelor's degree from Thomas Edison State University. He commenced his writing career at the age of forty-three. This being his first published book. He plans to let the public see more of his material, which will be eagerly anticipated, judging from *Trapped By Impulsion-* a tough, no-holds-barred, and thoroughly uncompromising debut.

Milton Keynes UK
Ingram Content Group UK Ltd.
UKHW030655170824
447045UK00001B/174